Fis'

A Rainey L...

by
Kathleen Suzette

A Gracie Williams Mystery Series
Pushing Up Daisies in Arizona,
A Gracie Williams Mystery, Book 1
Kicked the Bucket in Arizona,
A Gracie Williams Mystery, Book 2

A Home Economics Mystery Series
Appliqued to Death
A Home Economics Mystery, book 1

Table of Contents

Chapter One

"WE'RE GOING TO CATCH our death of cold out here," I said, trying to keep the whine out of my voice. The sun was just starting to peek its head over the horizon and the blowing wind had my nose running. I rubbed the back of my gloved hand beneath it. I wasn't a morning person under the best of circumstances.

Cade chuckled. "You'll be fine. As soon as the sun is up, you'll warm right up." He hefted the ice chest from the trunk of his car and set it on the frozen ground. "There's nothing like time spent in the great outdoors."

"I don't think I'll warm right up," I grumbled and picked up the two canvas folding chairs from the trunk. It was early January in Idaho and all I wanted was to hide beneath my electric blanket and sleep the morning away. A girl could dream, right?

"Come on, be a trooper. I know you can do it," he teased and led the way to the edge of the lake. "We'll have a mess of fish caught before you know it and then you can stand in front of a roaring campfire and fry them up for us."

"Yeah, that sounds like fun," I said and yawned.

"At least the fire will warm you up," he said over his shoulder.

I stumbled after him, my thick layers of clothing making me feel less than graceful. We stopped at the edge of the frozen lake and Cade looked it over.

"What if it doesn't hold us?" I asked. I had never been ice fishing, and I didn't think I would enjoy it. Mostly because it involved ice and bitterly cold temperatures. I had spent all of my life in snowy areas, first Idaho, then New York, and now back to Idaho, but I had never really embraced cold weather activities. At least, not when they occurred outdoors.

"It'll hold. I hear there've been a lot of trout pulled out of this lake this season." He set the ice chest down and headed back to the car for his fishing equipment.

I unfolded the two chairs and set them on the ground, then sat down in one. I pulled my knit hat down lower over my ears and re-wrapped my scarf. My eyes began to tear up from the wind and I blinked to clear them and sniffed.

"Hey, what are you doing sitting down?" Cade asked, returning with a tackle box the size of a small safe, two fishing poles, and an auger to drill holes into the ice.

I looked up at him. "I like the feel of solid earth beneath my feet. I think we should fish from right here on the bank."

He chuckled and shook his head. "How are we going to do that? The lake's surface is frozen solid. You can't cast your line out and expect it to do anything other than bounce across the ice."

I shrugged. "Just drill a hole a couple of feet out. I bet I can cast the hook into it from here."

"If I drill a hole a couple of feet from the bank, the water beneath it will only be a few feet deep. The fish aren't hanging out in the shallow water just waiting for us to catch them. Where's your sense of adventure?"

"My sense of adventure abandoned ship when it saw we were headed out into the cold. What if the ice doesn't hold us? I've seen videos of people falling through the ice and freezing to death before they can climb out," I protested.

"You've seen real people die in these videos?" he asked skeptically. "Or are you talking about when you watched *Titanic*?"

"I am not talking about *Titanic*. I saw real people. I guess they probably didn't actually die, but did you know you can freeze to death in icy water in less than fifteen minutes?"

He laughed and shook his head, taking a few steps out onto the ice, then bent over and used the manual auger to quickly drill a hole. "There. See? The ice is nice and thick. Come on out and bring those chairs. I've got ice to drill and fish to catch."

I sighed, got to my feet, and folded the chairs up again. The ice did look thick, and it wasn't that I doubted Cade, but I didn't like the idea of walking out onto that ice. Cade had bought me a pair of ice boots so I wouldn't slip, and I had put on two pair of socks to keep my feet warm, but they weren't working very well. My feet were freezing. I had also worn two layers of thermals beneath my clothes and I felt like the kid on *A Christmas Story* when his mother made him wear that absurd snowsuit. I drew a line at the ridiculous looking bib overalls Cade was wearing. They were bright orange and apparently waterproof. A girl's got to keep her sense of fashion even when ice fishing.

I looked up as Cade continued walking further out onto the ice. "Hey! Don't go so far out."

He turned and waited as I gingerly made my way onto the ice. I paused at the hole he had just drilled and looked into it. The ice appeared to be at least four inches thick. I strained my ears for cracking sounds, but the ice was blessedly silent.

"Come on. The big fat fish are out in the deep," he called. "I want to catch the really big ones. Go big or go home."

"I'll take little skinny fish if it means I can stay on the shore," I said as I braced myself and headed slowly in his direction. "Going home now would be even better."

"Live a little, Rainey. Look on the bright side. If we do fall in, you'll have something to tell our grandchildren."

I gasped and looked at him, then looked back at my feet. I didn't have any children, let alone grandchildren. Cade and I had only been dating a few months, but I had never been so happy in all my life. I had come off of a nasty divorce a year earlier and I swore I would never fall in love again, and yet, here I was. Not that I was admitting I was in love. Not yet, anyway. But sometimes, out of the blue, Cade would say something like he had just said, and I'd think, this is it. This is the real thing. The love I have waited for my whole life. As these thoughts passed through my mind, my foot slipped on the ice and I gasped again and put the folding chairs down on the ice, using them as a crutch to keep me upright.

"You okay?" he called. He had ventured further out onto the ice and I wished he would just stay put.

I looked up and smiled as the sun rose behind him. He looked stunning in the early morning light, silly overalls and everything. "I'm okay."

I made my way out to where he had set the tackle box down and begun drilling a hole in the ice. Unfolding the chairs, I set them several feet away from the hole. I had visions of my weight adding to the stress of holes being drilled into the ice and my ever-creative imagination saw us both falling into the treacherous water beneath the ice.

He glanced at me. "I can't sit in the chair with it so far way." He moved over to a spot about eighteen inches from the hole he had just drilled and made another one. The auger was amazingly quick in drilling holes into the ice.

I scooted the chairs closer once he was finished with the second hole. "We could just go to the grocery store and buy some fish."

"Once again, where's your sense of adventure? Besides. I bought these spiffy overalls. It would be a waste of money not to wear them."

"Yeah, I can see why you'd want to wear them. Everyone from Sparrow to Boise can see them."

He snorted. "These overalls are like your little black dress on date night. Would you want to dress up and stay home where no one can see you?"

"Well, when you put it like that," I said and sat down on my chair.

"Exactly. Now, what kind of bait would you like on your hook? I've got big fat nightcrawlers, minnows, and stinky marshmallows."

I looked at him. "I don't want to appear to be a greenhorn, but are the nightcrawlers and minnows alive?"

"Of course. The fish like their breakfast to have a little game. Makes them friskier." He opened his tackle box and began sorting through it.

"I was afraid of that. I'll take stinky marshmallows." I sat back in my chair and watched the sunrise. It was eerily quiet out on the lake and if it hadn't been so cold, I might have enjoyed it.

"I'll bait our hooks and then go get the ice chest," he said as he removed the lid from a jar of fluorescent pink marshmallows.

I peered at the ice beside me. The wind had blown most of the snow off of the lake's surface and I could see through it. It was a little unnerving as I saw what looked like a fish dart beneath me.

"This is really weird," I said. "What if I fall through the ice? I mean, seriously. Do we have a plan?"

"Stop it. You aren't going to fall." He handed me the baited fishing rod. "Now, all you really have to do is put the hook into the hole and wait for the fish to bite. Maybe move it around a little. I put a float on it. Trout like to stay somewhat near the surface and like to see their food float. I'll be right back."

I watched as he headed back for the rest of our equipment, then turned back to the hole in the ice. I got to my feet and peered into it, trying not to get too close to the edge. A small fish darted across the opening and I jumped a little. If Cade thought he was going to get nice fat fish, he might be mistaken. The two I had seen so far were far from large. I dropped the hook into the water, releasing some line, then scooted back to my chair and sat and waited.

Chapter Two

"SO, AGAIN, HOW DOES fried fish for breakfast sound?" Cade asked me. "I brought a little hibachi barbecue, charcoal, and a skillet. We can have a feast right on the bank of the lake."

I scrunched up my nose, my eyes still on my line. "I'm not sure fish sounds very good for breakfast. Lunch or dinner, yes. But I've never had it for breakfast."

"It would make a great recipe for your cookbook. Americans have been fishing and cooking up their breakfast near lakes and rivers for centuries. It's very rustic."

"Yeah it would be a great recipe for my cookbook, but not for breakfast," I said firmly. I was writing an Americana themed cookbook and while ice fishing was definitely an American pastime in states where it snows, I still didn't think I could stomach fried fish for breakfast.

He made a sound of disapproval, then handed me a thermos of coffee. "Maybe this will cheer you up. At the very least, it'll warm you up."

"Mmm," I said, brightening, and took the thermos from him. "I'm so glad you thought of coffee. I was just daydreaming about coffee and realized I hadn't thought to bring any."

"I took the liberty of adding cream and sugar to it when I made it," he said, baiting his hook with a minnow.

I looked away. I didn't have the stomach for fishing. The stinky marshmallows were all I could handle. Steam poured out of the top of the thermos when I removed the inner plug and poured coffee into the cup that came with it. My father used to take a big thermos of coffee with him to work every morning and I suddenly felt nostalgic. "This smells so good," I said and took a sip. The warmth was heavenly on this cold morning. I watched as a fish darted beneath the ice near my feet. It still gave me the willies to see them swimming so close to me.

"There's nothing like hot coffee on a cold morning. How's the cookbook coming, anyway? You haven't talked about it much lately."

I shrugged. "I got a little behind on it over Christmas, but I've been sending out book proposals to agents. Hopefully I'll hook one pretty soon. Get it? 'Hook'?" I chuckled at my own joke.

He snorted and shook his head. "You're too cute."

I looked over at him. His dark brown hair shined in the early morning sunlight. "You're pretty cute yourself."

He glanced at me and opened his mouth to say something, then turned back to his fishing line when the pole suddenly jerked in his hand. "I think we've got a winner. Come to Papa."

He jerked back on his rod, then began to reel the line in. The fish pulled on its end of the line and Cade jerked the rod back again.

"I think it's a big one," I said. The tension on the fishing line was robust as Cade continued to reel it in.

"You may be right," he said, getting to his feet. He took a couple of steps back and continued to crank the handle on the reel. After a couple of minutes, the fish came to the surface of the water and Cade took hold of the line, pulling it out of the hole in the ice. "Tada!"

"That's a big one all right," I said, standing up as the fish danced on the line.

The fish was large enough to feed several people. It suddenly occurred to me that someone had to scale and gut the fish, and I knew it was not going to be me. I drew the line at cooking it.

"Breakfast," he said sounding self-satisfied. "There's nothing like fresh fried fish in the morning."

I sighed and turned away as he removed the hook and put the fish into the bucket he had brought. "I'm really not feeling it, Cade," I said. "In fact, I'm feeling a little nauseous at the thought."

"What do you mean? Are you getting sick?" He looked at me, concern showing on his face.

"I mean I'd rather buy my food at the grocery store where I don't have to think about it ever having been alive." I took another sip of my coffee. It was cooling down quickly out in this cold weather. If I didn't drink it right away, I was going to have iced coffee.

He arched one brow. "You do know that all meat was alive once, right? Even the stuff you get at the grocery store?"

I rolled my eyes. "Yes, and I do like meat. But I don't like this," I said, indicating my fishing pole. I didn't have the heart for it. Let people who had grown up on farms and who liked to hunt and fish catch all the food. Grocery stores were for civilized people.

He sat back down and put more bait on his line. "It's okay. You don't have to look at the fish. I'll handle it. We can go get pancakes for breakfast when we're done."

He sounded a little disappointed, and I felt bad. I had put a damper on things. "Sorry," I said. "I'm not good at this kind of thing."

"It's okay. I may dress in a suit for work on most days, but I'm an outdoorsman at heart. Everyone isn't, and that's fine. I do appreciate you coming with me this morning."

"I like spending time with you," I said and shivered as a breeze blew across the lake. The cold was starting to sink into my body and my feet felt numb in spite of the wool socks and special boots. I didn't want to be a spoilsport; I just wasn't an outdoor kind of woman. I decided that if I moved around a little, I might be able to get warm, so I got to my feet.

"Where are you going?" he asked, putting more bait on his hook.

"Just trying to wake up my feet." I took a couple of stiff steps away from my chair. My feet felt like blocks of ice and my joints protested the cold.

"Be careful about not falling through the ice," he said without looking at me.

I narrowed my eyes at him. "I thought you said it was safe?"

He shrugged. "You never know," he said innocently.

I ignored him and took several more steps away from my ice hole. I was beginning to adjust to the fact that I was able to see beneath the ice and it was fascinating. Three fish came to the bottom of the ice where I was standing, then darted away. I wondered if they were cold. Did scales protect them from freezing? Did some of them hibernate in the cold? I was clueless.

I took a few more steps and there was a large school of fish that formed a dark shadow beneath the ice. When I got closer, they scattered, revealing murky water and what looked like seaweed.

"What is seaweed called when it's growing in fresh water?" I called over my shoulder.

He chuckled. "There are all different kinds of weeds that live in lakes. But no seaweed."

"I'd hate to swim in this lake in the summer," I said, carefully watching where I was stepping.

"Why?"

"I never swim in water I can't see clearly into. You never know what lurks in the depths. And the fish might bite," I said. The lake was huge, with public access in the area where we had come onto it. On the far side of it were a handful of houses that had docks. The owners usually had small boats anchored during warmer weather, but with winter in progress, the boats were nowhere to be seen.

"The fish will only nibble your toes. There's nothing to worry about," he said, raising his voice a little so he could be heard. "Are you going to walk across the entire lake?"

"Maybe. You said it was safe," I pointed out.

"Why don't you come back?" he said casually.

I stopped and looked over my shoulder. I had gone farther than I realized. Watching the fish scatter as I walked had been mesmerizing. "Why? It's safe, isn't it?"

"It's safe over here. I haven't gone out where you are to check the ice. I'd hate for you to fall through and freeze to death. It can happen in less than fifteen minutes, mind you."

I narrowed my eyes at him. He did have a point though. Did lakes freeze from the center out, or from the edges near the land and spread inward? I had no idea and suddenly the thought of the center of the lake not being frozen as solidly as the water near the bank where we had entered sent a chill down my spine. I carefully turned around so I could slowly make my way back toward Cade.

As I turned, I saw something red beneath the surface of the ice from out of the corner of my eye. It was off to the side and not directly beneath my feet. My first thought was that it was a fish. My second thought was that the color was too bright to be a fish. I took a few steps toward it, wondering what it could be. When I was over the top of it, I realized that it had to be an article of clothing, but I wasn't sure what kind. Maybe someone had lost a swimsuit or towel during the summer and it had been brought to the surface by some rambunctious fish.

I bent over to get a better look. "Hey Cade, there's something down here."

"What?" he called, his eyes still on his fishing pole.

I squinted my eyes. "There's something over here," I said, but the wind blew my words away.

"What?" Cade shouted. "What did you say?"

"There's something in here—." And that was when I screamed.

Chapter Three

I'VE GOT TO HAND IT to him—Cade can really move when the situation warrants it. He was by my side before I could catch my breath and scream a second time. I felt him more than I saw him because my eyes were glued to whoever was beneath the ice.

"What is it—oh," he said as he peered through the ice. He squatted down for a closer look.

"Is that what I think it is?" I asked, taking a step back. The shock of seeing a body beneath the ice made me hope I was imagining things in spite of what was obvious.

"Looks like it," he said slowly, not taking his eyes off the red beneath the ice. He brushed some loose snow away to get a better look.

"I told you the ice would break! I told you! Someone fell through the ice, didn't they? Is it a man? It's a man, isn't it?" I was suddenly babbling as panic set in. I kept backing up, unable to take my eyes off what looked like a red shirt beneath the ice. The ice had cracked and some poor soul had slipped beneath it, unable to pull himself out of the freezing water. I was sure that was it.

Cade looked up at me. "Rainey."

"I told you we shouldn't have come out here on this ice! You can freeze to death in cold water in less than fifteen minutes! I told you! I told you!" I continued backing away.

"Rainey," Cade repeated calmly. "Rainey, will you stop?"

"I want to go home! How are we going to get him out of there? Is it a him? I can't tell. How are we going to get him out of there? Oh my gosh, what if it's a her? What if she has children sitting at home and wondering where their mother is?" I was in a full-blown panic now and all I could think of was how awful it must have been to fall through the ice and freeze to death. What goes through your mind when you know you're about to die?

"Rainey," Cade said gruffly. "Rainey! Stop! Do you want to fall through the ice, too?"

That brought me to my senses. Sort of. I looked down at my feet, sure I was going to see an enormous crack already forming in the ice, but it was solid beneath my feet. I looked at Cade again. "Are we going to fall in?" I whimpered.

"No, but you're backing up without looking where you're going. Walk back toward me. You shouldn't go that far out." He pulled his phone from his pocket and made a call to the police department.

I walked forward, trying not to look at the red shirt, but I couldn't help myself. I stood next to Cade and looked with one eye open. Thankfully, whoever it was, was face down. All I could see was short dark hair, and I was guessing it was a man from the person's build. I shivered. What a terrible way to go. I hoped it didn't take the full fifteen minutes for him to die. The thought of the things that must have gone through his mind in his last minutes made me light headed and I looked away.

When Cade finished calling the incident in, he hit end on his phone and tucked it into the front pocket of his overalls. He pulled a dark blue handkerchief from his other pocket and laid it on the ice over the body. "Come on, let's get our equipment and put it in the car."

He took my arm, and we carefully made our way back to our fishing rods. "Have there been any reports of missing people lately?" I asked him.

"Not recently that I can recall, but I don't usually handle that kind of thing unless they think there's foul play involved," he said as he braced me when I slipped a little on the ice.

"Do you think he could have been in the lake long? Maybe he hasn't been missed yet," I wondered. My mind was turning with possibilities as to what might have happened.

"It's possible. The ice is pretty thick, but he might have found a spot that wasn't as solid as the area we've been walking on."

"How terrible. Maybe he's been in the lake for months. Or years. Is that possible?" I asked, horrified.

He shrugged and chuckled. "That imagination of yours. Let's take one thing at a time. We've got to get him out of there before we know anything conclusive."

"No, seriously. Is that possible? Could he have been in there for years?"

"I don't know all the particulars on dead bodies in water and decomposition rates, but the lake has been frozen for a couple of months, so I would think the body has been pretty well preserved if it's been in there awhile."

We went back to our chairs and equipment and began collecting everything. I looked into the bucket at the single fish Cade had had time to catch. It swam around in the water in the bucket, seemingly none the worse for wear after having been caught and hoisted rudely from his home. And then I had a gruesome thought. I gasped and turned to Cade. "Throw that thing back!"

"What? Why?" he asked as he closed the lid on the tackle box.

"Because it's probably been feasting on our friend in the red shirt!" I stared at him wide-eyed. The thought was enough to make me lose my breakfast if I had had any.

He tilted his head back and laughed uproariously.

"What's so funny? Why are you laughing?" I demanded.

"You! You have a wonderful imagination, Rainey," he said, shaking his head.

"I'm glad you think this is funny, but it isn't. I am not eating that thing!" I insisted. "Throw it back!"

"You don't have to eat it," he said and picked up the fishing rods.

"You're not eating, it either! That's disgusting!"

"Stop it, Rainey. It's just a fish," he said, still chuckling.

"I can't believe you would even consider eating it. If you do eat it, you can't kiss me, for like, a couple of months," I warned.

He shook his head. "Oh Rainey, it's better that we don't know what our food has eaten before we eat it. Honestly, you have no idea what the meat in the grocery store has done before it was turned into meat."

"Don't make me get mean about it," I warned.

He laughed again and went to the bucket. "Goodbye, breakfast." He poured the contents of the bucket including the fish back into the hole he had pulled it out of. Then he turned to me. "There. Happy?"

"Immensely," I said and picked up the chairs. We headed back to the car to wait for the police to show up.

"One of these days I'm going to catch some fish that I don't have to throw back and you're going to fry them up for me," he said wistfully.

"One of these days," I promised.

"Will you make me some fries and coleslaw to go with them? And hushpuppies?"

"I love hushpuppies. I haven't made those in years," I said as my stomach growled. I needed to get something to eat.

"SO, WHAT DO WE KNOW?" I asked as I handed Cade a cup of cocoa and sat beside him on my sofa. There was a fire roaring in the fireplace and the room was nice and cozy. My Dog, Maggie, lay snoring in front of the fire, her side rising and falling with each breath. Maggie was a Bluetick Coonhound, and she had rescued me from a killer several months ago. She could laze around all she wanted after that.

With the help of my mother, I had bought a cute little cottage several months earlier and Cade had helped me restore the hardwood floors to their original beauty. And by helped,

I mean that he did nearly all the work. They gleamed in the firelight and I pulled a throw blanket over the two of us. "Now, this is what I call a day off."

He took a sip of his cocoa and one eyebrow arched upward. "Day off? I spent most of it out in the freezing cold, watching as a team of police officers cut a huge hole in the ice on the lake and pull a dead man out."

"You weren't worried about freezing weather when you were killing fish," I pointed out.

"I killed zero fish. And we don't know much yet. Greg Barnes said he thought the dead guy is Rob Zumbro, but we'll need next of kin to identify him."

The name sounded familiar, but I couldn't come up with a face. "Was a missing person report filed?"

"Nope. I stopped by his house to speak to his wife, but no one was home. I'll try again when I leave here, and if she still isn't home, I'll try in the morning. He lives in one of those houses on the far side of the lake."

"Ah, that might explain a lot. I bet he had a habit of going ice fishing and he fell through. It's weird his wife didn't file a missing person report, unless it happened within the last day or so."

"He looked like he had been in the water for a while," Cade said. "And he wasn't dressed for ice fishing. That red we saw was a light nylon windbreaker."

"Ew," I said. "I told you that fish had been feasting on him. He didn't have his wallet on him?"

He shook his head and took another sip of his cocoa. "No personal effects on him."

"Hmm, that's odd," I said thoughtfully. "Don't you think that's odd? Men usually carry their wallets when they leave the house."

He snorted. "It's odd that he died out in the cold and no one reported him missing. And I do have my wallet on me when I leave the house, but I don't know if every man does. It might not have been unusual for this guy. Or his wallet may be at the bottom of the lake."

I nodded. I wouldn't be a bit surprised if his wallet had slipped out of his pocket while he was in the lake. It would be lost forever.

"Well what about his house? Did it look abandoned? Who is he married to? Maybe she left him and that's why no one knows he's missing. Maybe he's been in the lake for months and if she left him, maybe there wasn't anyone to report him." I thought I was becoming a good detective if I do say so myself. Cade wouldn't admit it, but I was his ace in the hole.

"That imagination of yours is in overdrive," he said and turned the television on. "Let's watch pro-fishing."

I groaned. He was going to have me stinking like an old dead fish if it was the last thing he did.

Chapter Four

CADE SQUINTED HIS EYES at me as I headed up the walkway to the Zumbros' house. "What are you doing here?" he asked.

I smiled at him. "I came to assist you. I've been thinking about Rob Zumbro all night. I couldn't sleep a wink, so I stalked his social media profiles. There are pictures of him with a woman I assume is his wife. She looks familiar, but I can't place her. I just don't understand why someone didn't report him missing."

He glanced at the house, then looked at me. "This is official police business. You don't belong here, Rainey," he hissed.

"I know, I know. I'm sorry. I probably shouldn't be here, but you know how I am. I need to know."

"You're *nosy*," he said emphatically. He was dressed in a casual wool suit today. The sun was up and shining, and it was surprisingly warm when it was directly on me, but a cold breeze sent a chill through my body. A wool suit was a good choice.

"I am not nosy. I want to help," I whispered.

Cade opened his mouth to protest again, but the front door to the Zumbros' house swung open, interrupting him. We both turned and looked.

The woman standing at the door had blond hair and was a little taller than my 5'4" height. She was the woman I had seen in the pictures online. She looked to be about my age, but I wasn't sure where I had seen her before.

"Can I help you?" she asked, looking at us uncertainly. Mrs. Zumbro, if that was who she was, looked like she kept herself fit. The leggings and t-shirt said we had interrupted her workout.

Cade forced himself to smile. "Good morning," he said and headed up the three porch steps, one hand extended.

Before he could get anything else out, she shook her head. "I'm sorry. I'm not buying anything, and I already have my own religion. I don't like solicitors."

She began to shut the door when Cade cleared his throat. "Mrs. Zumbro?" he asked. She hesitated, and I took that moment to follow Cade up the steps. I stood beside him like I belonged there.

"Yes, I'm Mrs. Zumbro. Why? Who are you?" Her eyes went from Cade to me and I smiled what I hoped was a comforting smile. She was about to get some terrible news and I hoped she wouldn't hate us for it.

"Mrs. Zumbro, I'm Detective Cade Starkey. I'm with the Sparrow police department," he said, sounding business-like. "I need a moment of your time to speak with you."

Her eyes took on a look of suspicion as Cade removed his badge from inside his coat and showed it to her. She relaxed when she saw it and then she glanced at me but didn't ask who I was. "Yes? What can I help you with?" she asked Cade.

"May I—I mean, may we come in?" he asked.

"Who's she?" she asked now.

He glanced at me, looking perturbed. "This is Rainey Daye. Mrs. Zumbro, may we come in for a moment?"

"Rainey Daye? Didn't I go to school with you?" she asked, peering at me. "I thought you looked familiar. I'm Sarah. My maiden name was Shaw."

Recognition dawned on me. "Oh, yes. I remember you. I think you were a year ahead of me. You were on the debate team, weren't you?"

She smiled and nodded. "Yes, three years. Why don't you come in?"

I hated that Sarah Zumbro was suddenly delighted at seeing an old classmate since we had such terrible news for her. It had been years since I had seen her, but I hadn't known her well in school. She was one of the smart kids and being a year ahead, I didn't hang around with her crowd.

She showed us to the couch in the living room and we took a seat. I inhaled deeply, bracing for what was coming and now regretting that I had taken a drive down here this morning. In the night I had decided the story I had made up about his wife having left him was true, and I thought I was going to take a look around a vacant house, not deliver bad news to a very present wife.

"Mrs. Zumbro," Cade began gently. "Can you tell me, when was the last time you saw your husband, Rob?"

"Please, call me Sarah." Her brow furrowed and then she smiled. "I guess it was early September. Labor Day, in fact. Why?"

I tried to hide my surprise, but I was pretty sure I didn't do a very good job of it. Her husband had been missing for four months and she was sitting here smiling about it?

I think this news might have stumped Cade because he hesitated a few moments. "Can you tell me where you think he's been these past four months?"

Sarah looked confused for a moment. "Well, I think he's been out fishing. Why do you ask?"

I desperately wanted to look at Cade for his reaction, but I forced myself not to. Something weird was going on here and I didn't want to miss a bit of it.

"Fishing for four months?" he asked. The confusion was increasing.

She chuckled and nodded. "You know how those avid anglers are. They fish night and day. You can't keep them away from the water."

"Indeed, I love to fish myself," he said and turned his head just the slightest bit toward me, then turned back to her. "But four months seems like a really long fishing trip. Do you mean he was out on the lake here?" He pointed in the direction of the lake her husband's body had been pulled out of.

"What? No. He's been traveling all over the country and fishing. Well, I think he's really been staying around Idaho, and maybe Montana and Wyoming."

Cade was silent a moment before continuing. "Sarah, I have some bad news, I'm afraid. There was a body pulled from the lake yesterday and one of the officers thought it was your husband, Rob. We need you to identify the body. I'm very sorry."

Sarah stared at Cade. It was a moment before she spoke, "I don't see how that's possible. He's on a fishing trip. I'm sure he hasn't even been in the area in weeks. Months maybe." She looked at me, disbelief showing on her face. "He withdrew ten thousand dollars a few days before he left. He said he was going to buy an RV and drive around the country and fish the best waters America has to offer. He wanted me to go with him, but I'm not living in any RV."

"When was the last time you spoke to him? Did he give you his itinerary?" Cade asked.

She shook her head slowly. "No. I haven't spoken to him since September. I'm not sure exactly where he was headed."

"You haven't spoken to your husband in four months?" I asked. I didn't mean to say it, but it was out of my mouth before I knew it. It didn't make sense and I couldn't understand why she was being so calm about not seeing or speaking to her husband in months.

She looked at me, her face going pale. She nodded. "He always wanted to be a pro-angler. I told him it wasn't feasible. We had bills to pay. But Rob didn't want to grow up and—," she trailed off. She swallowed and continued, "I couldn't live in an RV. I have a job—I'm a teacher. That's why I stayed home."

"Didn't you think it strange that you hadn't heard from him since September?" Cade asked.

She nodded, her eyes going to her hands clasped in her lap. "We had a fight," she said, looking up at Cade again. "He insisted he could make it pro. That there would be endorsements and he could make a living that way. I thought it was idiocy. I guess I wasn't very nice about it, and we had a fight. He had inherited a large sum of money when his parents died and he wanted to blow it on fishing equipment and take a few years off work to try to make it big. It was a crazy idea." She shook her head and looked at me imploringly.

I nodded and smiled sadly, wishing I had something constructive to say. "I'm sorry," is all I could manage.

"You didn't think it was odd that he didn't call you during this time? Were you having marital problems before this?" Cade asked, still sounding confused.

She took a deep breath before continuing. "Yes, we were having some trouble, mostly money trouble. I wanted to pay off the house with the money he inherited, but he wanted to run all over the country and fish. But it wasn't like we were having terrible fights all the time. We just couldn't seem to agree on how to use the money. He stormed off, saying he was going to live his life the way he wanted. I thought he'd be back, but when I tried to call him on his cell phone the next day, it went to voicemail. I thought he was being childish, and that he would come around in a day or two. He didn't, and he never called me."

"Why didn't you report him as a missing person to the police?" Cade asked, jotting her story down in his notebook.

She sighed. "He was making regular withdrawals from his bank account. I'm not on the account, but I have his online password, so I check it regularly. It wasn't huge amounts of money, just a few hundred or a thousand dollars at a time. I figured he was doing what he said he was going to do. Fishing.

I thought he would come to his senses sooner or later and come home. Or at least call me." She looked at me helplessly.

Cade sat back on the couch, seemingly stunned by what she was saying. "So, no contact with him at all for four months?" he asked.

She shook her head and began to cry. "I guess you think I'm an idiot."

"I think I'm just a little surprised is all," Cade said.

I didn't blame Cade for being surprised. Who sat by while their husband disappeared without at least trying to find him?

"Does he have other family?" I asked her.

She nodded. "Yes, he has two older brothers and an uncle here in town. I know he has several cousins and aunts and uncles in neighboring states. That's why I thought he was somewhere nearby." She turned to Cade. "This body, did it—did he—drown?"

"We'll have to wait for the autopsy, but there was a head injury."

Her brow furrowed in thought. "Is it possible it happened after he fell into the water?" she asked.

"It's hard to say at this point. The medical examiner will need to take a look at him," Cade said gently.

"Didn't his family think it was odd that he just disappeared?" I asked.

That question ignited a fire in her eyes. "He didn't disappear—he went on a trip. Fishing. I asked his brothers if they had heard from him, but they said they hadn't." She snorted and sat back on the loveseat. "Like those two would tell me anything. We moved to this side of the lake to put a little distance between them and us. It's not much, but being out here feels like you're living out in the wild and it gave both my husband and me such peace of mind."

"Where were the withdrawals done?" Cade asked, sounding business-like.

"At both local ATMs and ATMs in areas where his relatives live. I figured his brothers were lying to me about not seeing him and that he was occasionally coming back to town and staying with them. He was stubborn, and I just knew he didn't want to admit to me that he was wrong about going pro."

"When was the last withdrawal done?" he asked.

"A week ago," she said. "In Billings, Montana."

He nodded. "We still need you to make a positive ID to make sure it's him. I'll set it up. Again, I'm sorry," Cade said.

She nodded and looked away. "If something happened to him. If someone did something to him—then you might speak to his brother Zack. He was always looking for a fight with Rob."

We stayed a few more minutes and then took our leave. Sarah seemed shaken with the reality of the death of her missing husband and I felt sorry for her.

Chapter Five

"THAT WAS WEIRD," I said to Cade. Since I had taken it upon myself to just show up at the Zumbros' house, we each drove our own cars and met at my friend Agatha Broome's coffee shop, the British Coffee and Tea Company.

"Indeed," he said, taking a sip of his coffee. "I wish you wouldn't just show up unannounced like that."

I shrugged. "Sorry. I really thought the house would be abandoned," I said and took a slug of my mocha latte. "But really, who isn't concerned when their husband just disappears for four months?"

"I don't know. It is weird," he agreed and glanced around the shop. "Where's our friend, Agatha?"

"I don't know," I said, "she's usually here. You didn't tell me Rob Zumbro had a head wound. Was it bad? Do you really think it's possible he got the wound after he fell into the water?" I wasn't going to let him change the subject before I got more information.

"No, I don't. You know how things move in water. There would be too much resistance unless he was thrown in there with a lot of force and I can't imagine what would do that. Unless a motorboat was involved."

"And a motorboat wouldn't be on the lake this time of year. What about if he slipped on the ice and hit his head? That could cause a head wound," I said as my imagination took hold again.

"And then the ice cracked, and he slipped beneath it and it froze over him?"

I narrowed my eyes at him. "It could happen. You never know."

He shrugged. "That would be some freak accident, but I guess everything is wide open right now."

I nodded. "I'm going with slipping on the ice. The ice cracked open, and he fell, hit his head, and slipped into the water. Eventually the ice would seal itself by melting and then refreezing."

"I'm so glad I have you around to tell me what I would never think of." He grinned. "But like I said, that would be a freak accident. Sarah is going to come down to the station later this afternoon and identify the body."

I winced. "I can't imagine having to do that with a loved one. Is she going to see his body? I mean, like up close and personal?" The thought made me nauseous.

He smiled. "No, we'll do it from closed-circuit TV. He's down at the morgue, and she'll be at the station."

"What if she wants to see his body in person?" I asked. "I could definitely see someone wanting to do that. I couldn't do it, but I could see someone else wanting to do it."

He chuckled. "That mind of yours is something else. If she really wants to see him, she can. But I would suggest she wait until the funeral director does his magic. A body that's been in the water for four months isn't pretty."

I sighed. "When do we go and talk to his brother, Zack?"

"We don't. I will, but you won't." He took another drink of his coffee.

I sighed again, this time with a little more flair so he'd know I was annoyed. "You know I'm going to ask around about Rob and what he was up to before he disappeared, and you know you like it when I do."

He chuckled, and we looked up as Agatha walked into the coffee shop. She spotted us immediately and headed over. "There you two are! I was wondering where you'd gotten off to. It's been at least a week since you stopped by. My feelings are hurt." She pulled up a chair and sat down.

"You're exaggerating. We were here on Friday," I reminded her.

She laughed, "Oh, you. You know I can't remember a thing. I think I'm getting old."

"Nonsense. You don't look a day over twenty," Cade said.

She looked at him and brushed away the comment with her hand. "This one's a keeper, Rainey," she said to me. I didn't know exactly how old Agatha was, but I thought she must be at least in her early seventies. She was a British transplant, but her accent was as clean and crisp as the day she landed in America.

"I agree," I said. "He's kind of cute and he does grow on you."
Cade chuckled.

"Tell me, you two," she said glancing over her shoulder. "I heard there were a number of police cars and an ambulance at the lake yesterday. What's going on?"

I glanced at Cade. "There was an accident," I said.

"Don't tell me someone fell through the ice? Those crazy ice fishers are always taking chances," she said and removed the purple scarf she wore. She folded it up and tucked it into her purse. "Those people should have their heads examined."

"See?" I said to Cade. "Everyone knows it's dangerous out there."

He snorted. "You lived to tell the tale. Quit complaining." He gave me a wink.

She eyed Cade, then leaned forward. "Who was it?" she whispered. "Someone we know?"

"On that note, I've got to get back to work," Cade said. He turned to Agatha. "We don't know anything definite yet." Then he looked at me pointedly.

"Goodbye, Cade," I said, suppressing a smile.

"Goodbye, ladies," he said and picked up his coffee, leaned over and gave me a quick kiss, and then headed for the door.

When Cade was safely out of the shop, Agatha looked at me. "Well?"

I felt guilty telling Agatha, but she was going to find out anyway. Even if she didn't get it from me, Sparrow was a small town and bad news traveled fast around here.

"We went ice fishing yesterday morning and there was a body beneath the ice," I whispered. "But you've got to keep it quiet for now. Cade will never let me help him on another case if he finds out I told you."

"You know I'll keep it to myself. Do you know who the victim is?"

I shook my head. "I really can't say. The next of kin still has to identify the body."

She thought this over. "Ice fishing is dangerous. I can't believe you agreed to go. I bet the poor fellow fell through the ice and it froze over the top of him." She shook her head sadly. "It's a shame. All in the name of catching a few fish."

"You know how those fishermen are," I said. "I told Cade we could just go to the grocery store and buy some fish fillets, but he insisted we catch the fish ourselves." I decided not to fill her in on the fact that the victim had a head wound. It was too early to know if he died as a result of that or drowned.

"Oh, look who's here," Agatha said.

I looked up as my mother walked through the door. "Hey, Mom," I said when she spotted us and headed over.

"Rainey Jane Daye, I can't believe I have to hear from a stranger that you had an accident out on the lake yesterday. Are you okay?" Mom scolded.

"I didn't have an accident," I said. "Who told you that?"

"Bernice Johns. She lives on the other side of the lake and she said she saw you and a handsome man ice fishing on the lake. She said before she knew it, a bunch of police cars and an ambulance showed up. Why didn't you call me?" She removed her scarf and hung it on the back of the chair Cade had just vacated and sat down.

"It was only two police cars and an ambulance, and I did not have an accident," I repeated.

"What happened? And where is that handsome man?" she said looking around the shop. "When is he going to marry you? I need another son-in-law. I love Bob, but I'd like to add Cade to my collection of sons-in-law. Or son-in-laws. However you say it."

"Stop it, Mom. You aren't getting a new son-in-law," I said and took a sip of my drink. Mom was determined that Cade and I should get married, but I wasn't rushing anything. I was enjoying dating Cade.

"She and Cade found a dead body beneath the ice," Agatha whispered. "But we have to keep it quiet."

Mom gasped and looked at me. "Is that true Rainey?"

I sighed. I didn't want to go into details about finding a dead body with her. She didn't always keep things to herself. "It's true, and it's also true that we need to keep it quiet. And no, I don't have any more information than that. I better get going. I've got an afternoon shift at Sam's." I got to my feet and picked up my coffee. In a situation like this it was best if I vacated the area, otherwise, my mother would hound me for details.

"Fine, you go to work and leave us hanging," Mom pouted. "You'll fill us in when you get more information, right?"

"No," I said. "I'll see you two later."

I headed out before either of them could say anything more. I worked part-time as a waitress at Sam's Diner and while the job didn't pay much, it helped and it was a convenient escape for me just then.

Chapter Six

"I'VE GOT A HOT ONE today," Bill Severs said from across the room.

I looked up from my computer. It was two days after we had found the body in the lake, and I was at my second part-time job at the local newspaper writing lifestyle articles. And while it was enjoyable, I hoped to be given juicer assignments at some point. "What are you talking about?"

He looked up at me and grinned. "There was a body found out at the lake and the boss just handed the assignment to me. I love writing articles like this. It's a real mystery how this guy ended up in the lake. It's a shame we don't have more opportunities to write articles like this."

I narrowed my eyes at him. "Yeah, it's a real shame more people don't die so you can write articles about it."

He laughed. "Rainey, you're a card. You know what I mean. Small towns don't give us nearly enough opportunity to write exciting news features. Don't you get tired of writing articles about matching your curtains to your throw pillows?"

I could have argued with him, but just then I was writing an article on household organization with a focus on getting rid of clutter. I sighed. That article he was writing should have been mine. I was an actual eyewitness. Or at least I was an eyewitness to finding the body. I looked at him again. "Who are you going to interview?"

He shrugged. "The police. The widow, if I can get her to open up. Maybe other family members." Bill was in his early fifties. He wore black thick-framed glasses and walked with a limp.

"Who discovered the body?" I asked. Surely he had to know, right?

"A cop. One of them was ice fishing on his day off," he said, and quickly jotted something down on a notepad. Bill was an okay guy, but right at this moment I was feeling a little jealous that he was going to take the credit on an article that I should be writing.

"Really? Just the police officer? It seems like there would be other witnesses. I wonder if there were other people at the lake fishing that day." I stared at him, waiting for his answer.

He shook his head. "Nope. The detective handling the case said he was alone."

I sighed. It figured. Cade wasn't going to let me get involved if he could help it. He sometimes didn't mind if I asked around, but lately he had become nervous about me getting involved with his cases. It may have had something to do with me almost getting my head blown off recently. But I wanted this article. "Bill, why don't you let me write that article? I'm dating Detective Cade Starkey, after all. I might be able to get some information out of him."

He looked up at me. "You are dating him, aren't you?" He shrugged. "What could you get out of him? He's a professional. He can't just give you inside information."

"I wouldn't be so sure. I have my ways. Let me have it," I said, a little too eagerly.

He laughed again. "Are you nuts? I'm not turning this article over to you. I live for this kind of thing."

"I'll trade you articles. You write mine and I'll write yours," I offered.

He looked at me and narrowed his eyes. "What article are you writing?"

I glanced at the Word document I had open on my computer. I was nuts thinking he'd trade me. "Home organization."

He looked at me blankly. Then he laughed so hard I thought he would fall out of his chair. "You're crazy. No way. Besides, our editor isn't going to like it if we trade articles. He hands out the articles to who he thinks will write it best. And obviously, he knows I'll write this one the best."

I sighed. If that were true, then I'd be writing articles about tossing unmatched socks and baking cookies for the rest of my life. Why had I thought I'd ever get a chance to write anything else?

"Tell me what you have so far?" I asked. Maybe Cade had given him more information than he had shared with me.

"They said the dead guy had some kind of accident and he had a bloody head injury. It's murder, you know," he said as he opened up a blank document. "I can feel it in my bones."

I didn't know why Cade might suggest it was an accident when he knew it was murder, but there wasn't any blood that I had seen and the head injury hadn't seemed that bad. Bad enough to kill Rob Zumbro of course, but it didn't look like it was a huge wound and the water would have washed away any blood. "Did you know the victim?"

He looked at me. "Rob Zumbro? I saw him around town sometimes. His parents owned the old leather repair shop that used to be on Blake Street in the seventies and eighties. Not much use for that kind of shop these days. Everything's cheap and disposable."

I could barely remember my father taking me into the leather repair shop once when he left off a pair of boots to be repaired. Bill was right. There wasn't much use for those kinds of shops these days. Today many shoes were cheaply made with synthetic materials and bought for a few dollars. Disposable, indeed. "When did it close?"

He thought about it. "I guess in the late eighties. Later the Zumbros opened up a gift shop, but it didn't last long. Seemed Christopher Zumbro didn't have a lot of direction in life. It also seems like there was another business sometime in the mid-nineties, but I might not be remembering it right."

"What kind of people were they? Rob's parents, I mean."

"They were nice. Sparrow was even more tight-knit back then than it is now. People knew each other real well. I think Rob and his wife Sarah inherited money from his parents when they died. Rob's uncle, Barron Zumbro, was a real hotshot in the seventies. He was on the high school swim team."

"Oh?" I asked. "I guess sports were big around here even then."

"You better believe it. Back then everyone said Barron was on his way to the Olympics." He opened an internet page and searched for frozen lake facts.

"Really?" I asked. "But he never made it?"

He shook his head without looking at me. "No, he went off to college and joined the Idaho State swim team, but he got into trouble."

He didn't elaborate, and I sighed. I was going to have to pry the information out of him. "What kind of trouble?"

He stopped what he was doing and turned to me. "It was the mid-seventies. You know how it was. The country had moved from the counter-culture of the sixties to the sit around and get stoned culture of the seventies." He chuckled. "He took it to heart and got in pretty deep. Stoned athletes don't do much, except get kicked off the team."

"That stinks. He threw away an Olympic dream for drugs?"

He nodded. "Yeah. It caused an uproar around here. Everyone had been watching him. The paper ran articles on his progress at the college swim meets. The buzz of Sparrow producing an Olympic athlete was deafening. When he got kicked off the team and eventually out of college, people took it hard, especially his parents."

"Wow. Can you picture the regrets he must have now?"

"Yeah, I bet it's pretty crushing. His father never recovered from it. I remember being at the local theater one Saturday evening and his folks had stopped in to watch *Jaws*. There they were, standing at the snack bar, and someone made a remark about what a loser kid they had raised. His dad got into a fistfight right there in the lobby." He chuckled and shook his head. "It was a sight. I was just a kid then, and I had never seen adults get into a fight like that."

I could just imagine it. The shame Barron must have suffered for having been kicked off the team, and then the shame of his parents when people looked down on them. I didn't think people were very understanding back then and I could see things getting bad for them.

"What happened when he moved back to Sparrow? Did he come back immediately after he was expelled from college?"

"No, I think it took him several years before he moved home. I was in high school by then, and I saw all the swim trophies in the display cases that line the main hallway there. I saw him at the drug store one night, and he looked awful. Skinny and haggard looking. His hair looked like it hadn't been washed or combed in weeks." He shook his head. "I just thought he was a pathetic loser. I told the coach I thought his trophies should be removed from the display cases because he was such a disgrace."

I thought that was a bit much to ask, but didn't say so. "What did the coach say?"

"He got in my pimply face and told me to shut up. He said the guy was a champion swimmer and no one could take that away from him. He won those trophies for the team fair and square and until I was prepared to win my own trophies, I better shut my trap." He looked at me and grinned sadly. "I was fifteen and I'll admit that back then I was clueless about what makes a winner. He was right. He won those trophies fair and square."

"How did Barron's brother and his wife die?"

"A big rig pulled out in front of them on the freeway and they slammed into the back of it. Happened about this time last year. There was ice on the road, and they couldn't get their car stopped in time."

"How awful. I hope Barron and his family made amends a long time ago," I said.

"I wouldn't know. Poor sap. If he could only have gotten his act together before he lost his physical ability, he might have turned it all around." He turned back to his computer.

It was a sad story, and I did have to wonder how his failure in college had affected him. He had lost his brother last year and now his nephew was gone. Things hadn't turned out well for Barron Zumbro.

Chapter Seven

THE FOLLOWING DAY I was working a shift at Sam's Diner and wiping down the front counter in anticipation of the end of the day. With the cold weather, people tended to stay indoors whenever possible and things had been slow. We'd get off work early today.

The bell above the front door jingled and Stormy walked in. "Hey, sis," she said, sitting at the front counter. "What's up?"

I smiled. Stormy and I were identical twins. We were thirty-six, and while some identical twins grew to look less alike than one another as they aged, we still looked enough alike that people still sometimes got us confused. "Hey Stormy. Not much. Stopping in for a late lunch?"

"Not really. I already ate, but I heard there was an accident out on the lake and I knew you'd have the scoop," she said and grinned.

I sighed and put my hands on my hips. "What is it with people? Just because I'm dating a detective, everyone thinks I know everything that goes on around here."

"That's because you do. It's okay if you can't say. Can I get a cup of hot tea? It's such a cold, gray day today," she said.

"You got it," I said and went to get her a cup of hot water and a tea bag. I had brought in some spicy and fruity teas in case our customers wanted something besides Lipton. As a diner, we didn't usually have anything fancy, so I decided to help out with that.

I brought the cup of water and an orange spice tea bag to her. "Here you go."

She nodded. "When do you get off?" she asked.

I glanced at the clock above the door. "Probably a half hour or so."

She nodded and dunked the tea bag into her cup. "So, are you allowed to talk about it?" she whispered.

I leaned on the counter. "Cade and I went ice fishing and there was a body under the ice. It's Rob Zumbro." I whispered the last part.

She thought about it. "I think he's the brother of Zack Zumbro. He owns the feed store."

"I heard he does have a brother named Zack, but I didn't know he owned the feed store. How do you know that?"

"The kids have two bunnies in the backyard. I buy their rabbit pellets there."

That got me thinking. "Do you know him well?"

She shrugged. "I don't think I'd say I know him well, but I know him well enough to say hello and ask how the kids are. He has two kids, one in Curtis's class and one in Brent's. His brother Kyle has three kids, two of which are in the same classes as Curtis and Brent."

"Are those bunnies in need of some pellets?" I asked her.

"No, we still have half a bag, why—oh." She smiled. "We're going to go investigating, aren't we?"

I shrugged. "We'll need to keep it to ourselves, but maybe we can get a little information from Zack."

WE PULLED UP TO THE feed store, and I looked the place over. I had never been inside, and I didn't know why. Maggie could eat like a horse, and I figured they had to sell dog food.

There was a giant fiberglass horse out front and an old-fashioned wooden wagon. The outside of the store was done in rough-hewn wood siding and it gave me a cozy feeling just looking at it. The Wild West had come to Sparrow, and I didn't even know it.

We stepped into the feed store and felt the warmth of an old woodstove that crackled with a log on the fire. "Wow, that feels good," I said. There was a calico cat curled up on a cushion in front of the wood stove and I smiled. How had I not ever been in here before?

"I love coming in here," Stormy said. "The wood stove and the feed smell so rustic."

I glanced around. We appeared to be the only customers in the store and I didn't see any employees around. "Where is everyone?" I whispered.

"They're usually around here somewhere," she said.

I followed her as we walked down one of the aisles that had bunny supplies as well as bird and hamster cages and feed. She picked up a small round salt-lick. "Spot loves these."

"I had no idea they had bunny treats," I said picking up a small package of dried carrot treats.

"They have all kinds of stuff that the kids insist the bunnies need," she said with a roll of her eyes. Stormy had five kids, and it never surprised me when she suddenly announced they had a new pet.

We heard shuffling steps coming toward us, and in a moment, a tall man in a black cowboy hat appeared at the end of the aisle. "Hello ladies, is there something I can help you with?"

"Hi, Zack," Stormy said. "I'm afraid the bunnies need treats." She held up the salt lick and the bag of treats I had picked up.

He smiled. "Bunnies have needs just like the rest of us." He looked at me. "I'm not the sharpest tool in the shed, Stormy, but I'd say you have a twin sister."

She chuckled. "This is my sister, Rainey. Rainey, this is Zack Zumbro."

He stepped forward, reaching his hand out to me. "Pleased to meet you, Rainey. Your parents must be creative folks. Stormy and Rainey."

"Oh, you have no idea. I think it was our mother's fault that our names are weather related," I explained.

He nodded. "I like it."

"How are you, Zack?" Stormy asked.

He grew somber. "Not great. I just found out my brother drowned in the lake."

"Oh, no," Stormy said. "I'm so sorry to hear that."

"I'm sorry for your loss," I added.

There was a tremble of his lips before he pressed them together to make them stop. Then he sighed. "It's kind of hard to process right now. I sure didn't see it coming, but maybe I should have."

"What do you mean?" Stormy asked.

He shrugged and looked away. "He's been missing for four months. I guess we all kept telling ourselves he was out enjoying himself and living it up. Only now we find out he's been in that lake. Iced over."

"Did the police say he's been in the lake all this time?" I asked. Cade hadn't told me whether they'd figured out how long he had been in the lake.

"I guess we don't know that for sure, but I think so. He never contacted either me or my other brother after he left, and that's unlike him." He shook his head again. "I don't know what I was thinking. I don't know why I didn't file a missing person report instead of listening to that wife of his."

"I'm so sorry," Stormy repeated. "Where did you think he was all this time?"

"He had it in mind to be a pro-fisherman. Can you believe that? It never made sense to me. If you want to know the truth, Rob was always a little on the lazy side and I think it was just some fantasy he got stuck in his head. Then he took off. His wife said he did exactly that and there was no need to worry."

I wondered who was making withdrawals from his bank account if Rob had really been in the lake since Labor Day. "So he never called anyone at all? Not even his wife?" I asked.

"She swears he didn't. She asked my brother Kyle and me if we'd heard from him, but we never heard a word. I kind of just assumed Kyle might be lying about not knowing where Rob was, but I didn't come out and accuse him of that."

"Why would you think that?" I asked. I picked up another box of bunny treats for something to do with my hands.

He shrugged. "He and Rob had troubles sometimes. Our parents died in a car accident and left the majority of their estate to Rob. Kyle was bitter about it, not that I could blame him. I'm not really happy about it myself. Rob was the youngest and the money shouldn't have been left to him. It never made sense to me."

"It would make me angry, too," I said. "Did you ever ask your parents why they left the money to Rob? I'm assuming they made their will known before they passed, I guess. Or was it a surprise?"

"Oh, no. We knew. I told them it was wrong. But my dad, he was something else. When he decided he was going to do something, he did it regardless of what other people thought about it." He looked down at the floor, the toe of one boot poking the corner beneath the merchandise shelf beside him.

"I'm sorry to hear that," Stormy said.

It did make me sad. Zack seemed like a nice guy and he was clearly hurting now, both because Rob was dead and because of the decision his parents had made about their inheritance. It would break my heart if my mother gave everything she owned to Stormy. There were a lot of emotions tied to things like that and I could see how it would stir up a lot of pain from the past if things hadn't been good in the family.

"Your parents gave all the money they had to Rob?" I asked to clarify. I couldn't wrap my head around it.

"No, they gave him about eighty percent."

"And the rest was split between you and your brother Kyle?" I asked.

He nodded. "And my uncle Barron. Uncle Barron was my father's only brother, and they gave him five thousand dollars."

I took this in. If the lion's share had gone to Rob, then the person that would inherit the money at the time of Rob's death was his wife Sarah, unless he had a will that stipulated something different. And Sarah had made no effort to report her husband as missing.

"Who get's the money when Rob dies?" I asked just to clarify.

He shrugged. "I suppose his wife. But I'm not aware of any will Rob might have had made. Even if he did have one, I doubt he would leave it to anyone other than his wife."

I nodded. "He was young and a lot of young people don't have wills drawn up."

"I'm pretty sure he didn't have a will," he said. The front door swung open, and he glanced in that direction. "Excuse me, ladies. I need to check on this customer. Let me know if I can help you with anything and I'll be right back."

Stormy turned to me. "If there's no will, then any property he owns will go to his next of kin. Next of kin is his wife."

"That's the truth," I said, watching Zack approach the customer that had just come through the door.

I was glad we had talked to Zack. It gave me some insight into the Zumbro family dynamic and it wasn't a good one.

Chapter Eight

"DO WE KNOW FOR SURE how long Rob Zumbro was in the lake?" I asked Cade.

He hesitated, fork halfway to his mouth. "The medical examiner said it would be hard to tell exactly because the icy water preserved the body. But, there was some indication it had been a lot longer than just a few days." He stuck the bite of macaroni salad into his mouth. Macaroni salad is as American as it gets and it would fit nicely into my cookbook.

I thought this over. I had just filled him in on what I had found out from Zack. It seemed like Sarah was genuine in her shock that Rob was found in the lake, but some people were great actors. She had admitted that she and Rob had had money problems and had fought over how to spend the money left to Rob by his parents.

"Was he dead when he went into the water?"

"My dear Watson, I don't know that yet. The results of the autopsy are not in yet," he said and took another bite of the salad. "This is really good. You should cook professionally."

"Funny," I said. "But you're treating this as a homicide, right?" I picked up my fork and took a bite. "Mmm, this really is good, if I do say so myself."

"We are treating it as a homicide because of the head wound. The medical examiner is highly doubtful that it was an accidental drowning or that he slipped on the ice. The wound is at the top of his head and he would have had to do a back flip or somersault or something similar to hit it at that angle."

"I knew it. Someone wanted that inheritance money," I said. "People are so greedy." I shook my head and took another bite of the macaroni salad.

He chuckled. "You knew it? You were the one that said the ice cracked and he hit his head and slipped beneath the water."

"Yeah, but I changed my mind two days ago. I just forgot to tell you."

He snickered, shaking his head. "You are something else. You don't get the recognition that you deserve. You're an ace sleuth."

"I really am. You should pay me a part of your salary for all that I do for you. I also have a date with my sister tonight. Guess where we're going to go?"

"No. Just tell me. And I'm not giving you any money."

"A high school basketball game," I said and stuck another forkful of the macaroni salad into my mouth. I had added tiny cubes of sharp cheddar cheese and finely chopped sweet pickles to it. My mom made something similar when I was a kid. She would probably want credit and royalties.

"Sounds like fun," he said. "I didn't think you liked sports."

I shrugged. "I don't. But my nephew Brent is playing. He's a sports nut and Stormy thinks Kyle Zumbro will be there. His son is on the team."

He gave me a lopsided grin. "So this date isn't just for fun. It's business."

I nodded. "You got it. Aren't you glad you asked me to ask around town and see what I could find out about the murder?"

"I only asked you to do that one time," he pointed out. "You're just nosy by nature and you enjoy sticking that cute little nose into everyone's business."

"You know what they say. Do what comes naturally to you. It's like I'm gifted or something."

I SCANNED THE CROWD for a tall man that resembled Zack Zumbro. Zack had to be at least 6'5" and I figured his brother had to have inherited some of that height.

Stormy leaned toward me as the basketball teams took to the court. "Are you looking for Kyle?"

I nodded. "Do you see him?"

"He's over by the snack bar." She pointed out a tall, dark haired man that was leaning against the wall.

I nodded. "Let's go," I said. We got to our feet as the crowd erupted in a roar at the announcement of the names of the home-team players.

As we approached Kyle, he smiled at Stormy, and then looked puzzled as he saw me walking behind her. I thought Kyle looked older than we were by a few years.

"Hi, Kyle," Stormy said when we got to him. "It's a good turnout tonight."

"Hi, Stormy, it is a good turnout," he said, and then looked to me. "How did I not know there were two of you?"

She laughed and introduced me. "I keep her a secret. That way she can fill in for me for various mom duties and no one's the wiser."

He grinned. "That's a great idea. Makes me sorry that I'm not a twin."

"Kyle, I just wanted to say that I'm so sorry to hear about your brother, Rob," Stormy said soberly.

"I'm really sorry for your loss," I added.

His mouth made a hard line, and he gave a quick nod of his head. "I appreciate that. It's a shock. I don't know what we'll do without him. He was the baby of the family." He looked away when he had finished speaking.

"Do they know what happened?" Stormy asked. "I saw Zack at the feed store and he said he died in the lake."

He nodded and turned back to us. "Yeah, but the police think someone killed him and put him in there." He sighed angrily. "I still can't process the fact that he's gone. Rob was kind of immature, you know? But I guess that was because he was the baby. Our parents didn't really expect a lot out of him. They spoiled him. I just don't know who would do this to him. He was a good guy."

"Did Rob have any problems with anyone?" I asked as delicately as I could manage.

"I don't know. Not that I can think of. Well, I guess I might be able to think of someone." He looked at me and then Stormy.

"My uncle Barron sure was mad when my parents left Rob the lion's share of their estate when they died."

"Why would he be mad?" I asked. I couldn't imagine why Barron Zumbro would be angry with his brother leaving his money to his own kids. It didn't make sense that one child got more than the others, but I couldn't see how it would concern Barron.

He shook his head. "I have no idea. It was a shock that they gave Rob most of the money. I mean, we knew about it before my parents died, but it never made sense to me. Sure, my parents favored Rob, but I never saw it coming. It's disgusting, to tell you the truth. But Barron, he was livid when he found out. He didn't know about it before they died. He found out about it at the reading of the will."

"Why would Barron think he should get part of their estate?" Stormy asked. "I can see where you and Zack thought you should get more of the inheritance, and you should have. You had every right to expect it."

"He said my dad had told him he would always take care of him. Honestly, it didn't make sense to me and I never heard my dad promise anything like that. My dad left him five thousand dollars and I think that was more than enough. Uncle Barron has always been one of those people that don't like to work much. My dad always said he never amounted to anything."

"Sometimes people think they're entitled to more than they are," I said thoughtfully. I had to agree with both Kyle and Zack. I would be hurt and angry at not getting an equal share of the estate, and I couldn't imagine why Barron thought he should have gotten more money than he did.

"That's just how he is. He wanted Zack to give him a job at the feed store a few years ago. Uncle Barron told him he could be the manager and asked for a lot of money to do the job." He chuckled. "My brother laughed at him. He runs the place himself."

I shook my head. Sometimes having a small family like mine was an advantage. We didn't have any kooky relatives waiting in the wings, hoping for something that they weren't entitled to.

"I heard Rob was missing for a while before his death," Stormy said.

"Yeah, he thought he could make a living from fishing. Can you imagine that? That guy was an idiot sometimes. I mean, how many people in this world actually make their living from fishing? I'm not even talking about people on commercial fishing boats. I'm talking about people that go out and fish for themselves. It's a hobby at best."

"It does seem like it would be kind of hard to make a living at it," I agreed. "I bet you were worried when he left."

"Not at first. After a month or so, I told Kyle we should have the police look into it, but he thought his wife Sarah was lying to us about not hearing from him. He thought Rob had to be checking in with Sarah. Even I thought it was weird that he wouldn't do that. It wasn't in keeping with his nature."

"He'd never done anything like that before?" I asked.

"Nope. I knew he and Sarah fought a lot, but I still didn't think he'd leave without getting in touch with her from time to time. Just disappear and not tell anyone where he was going? It didn't sound right to me."

"I don't think there are many people that would do that when they have families that care about them," Stormy agreed.

A sad look came across his face. "That's the truth right there. He did have a family that cared about him. We might not have been as close as the Waltons, and we do have our problems, but we would never just walk off and leave without letting someone know where we were. I really regret not reporting him missing to the police when he first disappeared."

I thought he was being genuine, but it still didn't make sense he nor the rest of his family hadn't been more concerned about Rob's disappearance long before his body was found in the lake.

Chapter Nine

"HEY RAINEY, WHERE'S our food?" Sam asked from his place by the grill. He had burgers on the grill and when the fat dripped down into the fire, the flame shot up from the bottom of the grill. He leaned back to keep from getting burned.

"Why, Sam Stevens, your food is right there on the grill in front of you. Careful you don't burn the burgers," I said, picking up a plate of deep-fried catfish and crispy fries for my customer at table one.

He chuckled. "You know what I'm talking about. It's been weeks since you made us something from your cookbook. I thought you needed our input. I'm a little hurt and disappointed."

"I do need your input, Sam. I've just been busy. I'll work on something for you." I headed out to the floor to serve my customer. I had been testing out my recipes for my cookbook on my co-workers and the customers. Sam was right. It had been a while since I had brought something in. I'd have to remedy that. "Here we are." I set the plate in front of Arnold Singer, one of Sparrow's friendliest mailmen.

"Thanks, Rainey. This sure looks good," he said, looking over the plate of food.

"It is good. Sam gets a shipment of freshly caught fish twice a week," I said and headed over to the front counter. Luanne had the rest of the tables and I had the front counter and table one. "Hi there," I said to the man that had just arrived and sat down at the front counter. "Do you know what you'd like yet, or would you like to look the menu over?"

He looked up at me and squinted his eyes. "Don't I know you?"

He was an older man with black hair that was graying around the temples. He did look familiar, but I couldn't place him. "I don't know, do you?"

"What's your name?" he asked, tilting his head in thought.

"Rainey Daye. What's yours?" I asked.

He chuckled. "That's it. I'd never forget a name like that. You and your sister were the cutest little girls. Of course, you were grown when I actually knew you, but I remember seeing the two of you when you were still in pigtails. Your mother loved to show the two of you off. Barron Zumbro." He stuck his hand out for me to shake.

My eyes widened, and not just because I knew some of his story. I didn't remember him and I wasn't sure why he would know who I was. And then it hit me. My father had passed away when I was nineteen and a year later, my mother had tried dating, at the urging of her own mother.

"You dated my mother, right?" I shook his hand and laid a menu down in front of him.

He chuckled. "I did. Your mother and I went out exactly two times, but then she decided I wasn't worth the trouble."

"Nonsense! If I remember right, she said you were a very nice man. She just wasn't ready to date after losing my father," I assured him. I could hardly believe I had forgotten that my mother had gone out with him. I hadn't put the name to the face, and if he hadn't remembered me, I might never have realized he was the man my mother had gone out with seventeen years ago.

"How is your mother?" he asked. "I see her around town once in a while, but I think it's been a least two years since I last ran into her."

"She's doing just fine. Still running the flower shop. You should stop in and say hello to her," I suggested.

He nodded. "You're right. It's not like I couldn't have done that. I haven't been in here in several years, either. I guess I just don't get around much. I really should stop in and see your mother," he said and then tilted his head again. "She still single?"

I chuckled. "As a matter of fact, she is." Barron was probably in his mid-sixties and was handsome. He looked like he was still in good shape and I wondered if he swam much these days.

He nodded. "I don't mean to sound impudent, but your mother was always a fine looking woman. She passed that on to her daughters."

I laughed. "Well, thank you. I'll tell her you said so."

"That would be nice," he said. "What have you been up to?"

"Well, I had a disastrous marriage that lasted ten years. Then I moved back to Sparrow from New York, and here I am."

"Well, you're single?" he joked. "Maybe I should ask you to dinner instead of your mother."

"I'd be flattered, but I am in a very committed relationship," I said with a chuckle. Barron had a way about him and even though he was much older than me, he managed to not come off as creepy.

He nodded. "I'd be setting my sights far too high, anyway. What's good today?"

"Sam just got some fresh fish in, and there's always the clam chowder," I suggested. "Neither can be beat."

He nodded. "How about the clam chowder since it's a cold day?"

"You got it," I said, jotting his order down on my order pad. I took it to Sam. "It's just clam chowder, Sam. I'll get it."

"Okey dokey," Sam said as he flipped a hamburger patty.

I got Barron his bowl of clam chowder and some crackers and took it to him. "Would you like something to drink?"

"No, this is fine," he said. "It sure smells good."

"It's the best," I said as I wiped down the far side of the front counter. I wanted to ask him about Rob, but I wasn't sure how to do it. I hung out around the front counter, hoping he'd want to make conversation. He seemed lonely, and I thought he might open up eventually.

After eating a couple of bites of the clam chowder, he looked in my direction. "Did you hear my nephew passed?"

I turned to him. "I did. I'm so sorry."

"They found him in the lake. I can't imagine what happened to him." He shook his head and looked at his bowl of chowder.

I sighed. "It's terrible. I know this has got to be so hard for you and your family."

He shrugged without looking at me. "I guess so. I don't have much to do with them. My brother, he was something else. Raised those boys of his to be just like him." He turned and looked at me now. "Proud of themselves, they are."

"I'm sorry. Do you have children, Barron?" Being alone must have made things even harder when family members died.

He shook his head. "No. I never married. I thought about it once. I dated Irene Black back in high school and I just knew she was the one. But, things didn't work out, and we went our separate ways. Irene was a looker." He chuckled at the memory and took another bite of his clam chowder.

"I'm sorry you aren't close to your nephews," I said.

"It's okay. Rob, he used to come around when he was a kid. He had a newspaper route, and he'd stop off when he delivered the paper. We'd talk. I did like that boy. I'd fix his bike when it had problems. Changed the tire or fixed the chain when it got a kink in it. Good kid."

He sounded sad when he talked about him. "I'm sorry," I said. "I'm glad you have good memories of him from when he was young." I couldn't think of much else to say.

He smiled at me. "He changed when he got older. Turned out just like his father. Selfish and greedy."

I was surprised at the sudden change in his tone. "Oh?" I said for something to say.

He nodded and looked away. "Served Rob right to marry that woman he married. She's something else, too. If you want to know the truth, it wouldn't surprise me a bit if they figure out she killed him."

"Why do you say that?" I asked him.

"She was tight with money. She wouldn't let go of a nickel if the Pope needed it to make a phone call to God himself." He chuckled. "They fought all the time. I heard it from Rob's brothers. They could hardly stand her. Said she tried to tear the family apart."

I shook my head slowly. "That's a shame. I'm sorry to hear that. Some people just aren't happy unless they can make others miserable."

"You can say that again," he said. "Maybe you could say I'm bitter, but I asked Rob for a thousand dollars so I could have surgery to have my gallbladder out. It was for my deductible and I just didn't have it at the time. I promised I would pay it back. Rob would have been okay with it, but she wouldn't let him give it to me." He snorted and shook his head. "Talk about tight-fisted."

"Wow, that's kind of cruel," I said. "But do you really think she could have killed her own husband?"

He nodded. "Sure do. Rob had some money put away and if he was dead, it would be hers. She wanted to open up a business, but Rob wouldn't let her. He even refused to put her name on the bank account the money was in because he knew she would spend that money if she had the chance. Seems she's only tight with money if it's hers. I heard from his brother Zack that she was livid when he refused to put her on that account. Said she'd pay him back."

"Really? She seemed so nice when we were in school," I said thoughtfully.

"Sure, but people change. You know how it is," he said solemnly. "Well, I don't mean to fill your head with negative family stuff. Maybe I'm just missing Rob. The Rob I knew when he was ten."

"I'm sorry," I said again.

It made me feel bad that he was alone in his grief. Even if he hadn't been close to Rob in recent years, he clearly had good feelings about their earlier relationship. And what he said about Sarah made me wonder about her. She had admitted they had money troubles and fought about what to do with the money Rob had inherited. It was something to keep in mind.

Chapter Ten

"SO WHAT'S NEXT ON YOUR list of things to fix?" Cade asked me. He was laying at one end of the couch and I was laying at the other, my legs draped over his. Maggie moseyed over and rested her head on my legs.

"Hey, you're too heavy," I said, rubbing her head. "I think we should do some painting. I didn't really notice how dingy the walls were until the floors were restored. Now it draws the eye to them instead of to these gorgeous floors." The floors really were beautiful. They had been a medium brown, but I had chosen a honey color to give the rooms a facelift.

He groaned. "I hate painting."

"Me too, but somebody's got to do it." I giggled and poked him in the ribs with my toe.

His phone rang, and he pulled it out of his pocket and frowned. "Sarah Zumbro." He answered it, "hello."

I watched his face as he listened. "I'll be right over. Thanks for the heads up." He ended the call and looked at me. "Seems Sarah just realized that Rob's boat is in the barn. She took a look through it and discovered his cell phone." He pushed my legs off of his and got to his feet. Maggie stepped back and gave a snort at being asked to move.

"I'm coming with you," I said, standing up and grabbing my coat from the back of the couch.

"I don't think that's necessary," he said, picking up his own coat from the couch back and putting it on.

"It may not be necessary, but I want to," I said and grabbed my purse. "See? I'm all ready to go. You don't even have to wait on me."

He sighed and headed for the door. "You are just an observer. I don't need your input."

"Got it."

IT WAS RARE FOR CADE to allow me to go with him on official business, so I was trying to be unobtrusive, but I was excited. Getting information first-hand was a treat. I normally had to slink around and get what information I could on my own.

"Hello, Detective, Rainey," Sarah said to us when she answered the door. "Come in."

We followed her inside, and she picked up a cell phone from the coffee table and handed it to Cade. "I can't believe I never looked in the boat." She shook her head. "I really don't have much reason to go out into the barn, so it didn't occur to me to look out there."

Cade looked at the cell phone. "I hope the weather hasn't ruined it. I'll take it with me to the station and see if there's anything on it that will help with the investigation."

"It needs to be charged, but I hope it will still work. I guess that explains why I couldn't get ahold of him when I called it." She sighed. "I know he kept it locked with a password, but I suppose you have someone that can figure that out."

Cade nodded. "We do. Can I take a look at the boat?" he asked her.

"Sure. It's just a small rowboat. Follow me."

We followed her out the door and down a narrow paved path toward a dark brown wooden structure that looked as if it had been built in the middle of the last century. The barn was small and filled with gardening tools, a tool bench, and the small rowboat. It was pushed up against a wall on the far side and covered with a blue tarp.

"During warm weather, we leave it tied to the dock. There are a couple of neighbor kids that like to borrow it to go fishing," she said.

Cade pulled the tarp back and looked into the boat. "Was the boat missing at any time right after Rob left?" he asked. I walked closer and peered into the boat.

"I honestly don't know. I have no interest in fishing, and like I said, the boys borrow it whenever they want. In late September, they brought it back and put it into the barn for me. They usually use it as late into the fall as they can before it snows, but they got into some trouble with their father and he grounded them and told them they couldn't fish the rest of the season."

Cade nodded and picked up a fishing rod that was lying on the bottom of the boat. "Does this belong to the boys or to Rob?"

She shrugged. "I couldn't tell you. I don't know one fishing pole from another." She looked at me and shrugged again. "I know nothing about fishing."

"I'm right there with you on that," I said. "I'm completely clueless."

Cade examined the rod and reel. "It's an expensive fishing rod. Orvis. This will set you back anywhere from several hundred bucks to a few thousand. I'd bet it was Rob's and not the kid's rod."

"That was Rob for you. He had to have the best," she said and rolled her eyes. It seemed even with his death, she was angry about his spending habits.

Cade looked into the boat again and picked up a tackle box. "What about this? Does this look familiar?"

She looked at it, then shook her head. "Nope. I'm afraid not."

Cade opened it. "Lots of lures. Nice ones. Might be Rob's if he liked to spend a lot of money on fishing equipment."

"So, Rob left on Labor Day," I said, trying to piece things together. "And you didn't hear from him again, right? Not even in the beginning?"

"That's right," she said. "Not a word. Like I said, I tried to call his cell phone, but he didn't answer. Now we know why, of course."

"And the kids were using the boat. So, how did they get the boat if Rob took it out on the lake? Wouldn't it have drifted off if he had had some kind of accident?"

"To be honest, I don't know if he even went onto the lake that day. I thought he did, but it's been so long ago, I'm not sure if it was Labor Day or another day. I'm sorry," she said. "I wish I could be more help."

It bothered me that now she was having trouble remembering which day her husband had been out on the lake where he had died. How hard would it have been for her to walk out here into the barn and take a look at the boat he would have been using before he disappeared?

Cade turned back to the boat. "It's not much of a boat, so I can see why he wouldn't want to take it with him if he had actually done what he said he was going to do. We still don't know if he was killed in the last few weeks or if it was months ago. How much money in total did he take from the account?"

The big question now was whether he had been killed four months ago or if it was more recent. There were too many holes in Sarah's story and I was sure I was looking at a guilty woman.

"Including the ten thousand before he left? Seventeen thousand. That's why I didn't really worry. The money was withdrawn a few hundred at a time, and twice it was one thousand dollars. I feel like a fool for not being more worried," she said. Her eyes welled up, and she blinked the tears back.

The tears made me doubt my assumption that she was guilty. I was a sucker for the waterworks. I wanted to tell her not to blame herself, but if I were in the same position, I would hate myself. Of course, I couldn't imagine not reporting a loved one if they had disappeared and not contacted me for four months.

"We're working on getting video from the banks where the ATM withdrawals were done, but that takes time. Without your name on the account as a joint owner with him, we have to go through the courts. If it wasn't him making the withdrawals, and he was in the water as long as we think he was, then I want to know who was taking that money out of his account," Cade said.

"I'd like to know, too," she said.

"I'm going to take the phone, the fishing rod, and tackle box with me. I'll send someone for the boat. Maybe there's something in here that will help. I'll also get fingerprints, but if the kids were using the equipment, their prints will be all over the place," Cade said, closing the tackle box.

"It's a terrible thought, but do you think the boys might have had something to do with his death?" I asked her.

"Oh, no. These are good kids. They're twelve and thirteen and are very responsible boys," she said.

I nodded. I hoped she was right. It would be beyond creepy if they had killed Rob and then used his boat and equipment while he lay at the bottom of the lake.

"Is there anything else you can think of, Sarah?" Cade asked her as he picked up the equipment and we headed toward the barn door.

"No. I've been racking my mind and I can't think of anything else. I appreciate all you're doing. The funeral is tomorrow. I just want it over and done with," she said. "It makes me sick that I didn't report him missing. I don't know what I was thinking."

"If you think of anything else, you'll let me know?" he said.

"Of course," she promised.

We headed back to Cade's car where he stowed the fishing equipment in the trunk, then we got into the car. I turned to him. "I can't get over her not reporting his disappearance. What about you?"

"I feel the same way," he said and started the car. He turned to me. "I can't imagine not being concerned about a missing loved one."

"Me too. And then there was what Barron Zumbro said about her being tight with money." I had already filled him in on my conversation with all three of the Zumbros. I didn't understand the lack of concern over a missing family member. They were all properly saddened that he had died, but why wouldn't they have looked more closely into the reason he had disappeared?

Chapter Eleven

"I NEED CAFFEINE," MOM said, leaning on the front counter at Agatha's. "I'll waste away to nothing if I don't get it soon."

"Caffeine doesn't have any calories or any kind of sustenance," I pointed out.

She gave me a sideways glance, then turned to the barista. "I'd like a large caramel mocha with a double shot of espresso, please. Smarty pants here will have water."

"I'll take a medium vanilla latte, please," I said. "She's being dramatic. I find it best to ignore her."

The barista grinned but didn't comment. Smart girl.

"If I'm being dramatic, that must be where you get it from," Mom said.

I snorted. "That must be it."

"Girls!" Agatha said, waltzing over to us. "I was just thinking how much I'd love to see the two of you today. It's like I'm psychic. Let me get my tea and we'll visit awhile."

"Hi Agatha," I said. "It has been too long."

"At least a day or two," Mom said.

Agatha cackled with glee and went behind the counter. She had a cup of tea already made and when the barista finished with our coffee, we headed to a corner table.

"Now, tell me. Where is that handsome man of yours, and how is the latest case coming along?" Agatha asked me after we had settled into our chairs.

"Yeah, what's going on with that?" Mom asked. "Seems like you'd keep your mother in the loop."

I took a sip of my coffee. "Cade is still working on it. I honestly don't have much information." I didn't want to give away everything I knew. Cade wasn't always generous with what he had learned about a case, and I didn't want to disappoint him by telling something that should be kept private. It helped that this time around I had been with him when he gathered some of the information, but I was going to keep as much of it to myself as I could.

Mom made a tsk–tsk sound of disapproval. "I know you know more than you're letting on."

"Actually, I do have something you might be interested in," I said. "I ran into an old boyfriend of yours. Well, I guess you might not call him a boyfriend since you only went out with him twice."

She looked at me expectantly. "Who?"

"Barron Zumbro."

Her eyes went wide. "I would definitely not call him an old boyfriend. He's not much more than an acquaintance."

"Why? What happened?" I asked.

She shrugged. "Nothing happened. I think it had only been a year or so after your father died, and I wasn't ready to date yet."

"I think I know him," Agatha said. "He was a big deal around here years ago, if it's who I'm thinking of, anyway. I didn't live here when he was the talk of the town, but I still heard all about him when I moved here in the eighties. I don't hear so much about him lately though."

"He was an Olympic contender," Mom supplied. "He was a nice guy. He was a little older than me, but I remember all the hoopla surrounding him when he went off to college, and then his downfall when he came back." She shook her head. "It's a shame things didn't work out. Where did you see him?"

"At the diner. He remembered me, but I didn't realize I knew him until he reminded me. So the only reason you stopped seeing him was because you weren't ready to date?"

"Mostly. But, I felt like he might still be drinking. Something wasn't right and I couldn't put my finger on it. You girls were older, but I guess I was missing your father. I decided it wasn't worth the risk." She picked up her coffee and took a slug of it. "Perfect."

"Have you ever thought you'd remarry?" I asked her. It was something I hadn't put much thought into. Dad had been gone for years and she had seemed content on her own. But maybe I was wrong in thinking she was happy.

She shrugged. "If I could find someone as attractive as Cade, I'd consider it. There wasn't anything wrong with Barron. Maybe I didn't give him a fair chance. I might have been making an excuse, thinking he might be drinking, on account of still missing your father."

I leaned forward. "Barron's the uncle of the guy we found in the lake," I whispered.

"Really? That's a shame," she said. "He's probably struggling with that now. Poor thing."

I nodded and looked at the front door. Sarah Zumbro walked in and headed to the front counter.

Agatha turned to see who I was looking at. Then she leaned in toward me. "Is that the widow of the fellow that drowned?"

I nodded and watched Sarah. When she got her coffee, she turned around to look for a table. I smiled at her and she met my eyes and smiled back. She headed over to me.

"Hi Sarah," I said. "Would you like to sit with us?"

"Hi Rainey, I wouldn't want to intrude."

"I was just getting ready to get back to work," Agatha said. "Why don't you have a seat?" She stood up and picked up her tea. "I'll talk to you ladies later."

I introduced Mom to Sarah and then Mom picked up her cup. "I should go too. I left the flower shop with my part-time help. She's new and I don't want to leave her alone long," Mom said.

"I guess I know how to clear a room," Sarah said when they had left and laughed.

I waved away the comment. "No, we try to get together several times a week. Sometimes it lasts a few minutes and other days it lasts a couple of hours."

"There's nothing like hanging out with family and good friends," she said with a sigh. "My family has gradually moved away from Sparrow over the years and I sure do miss them."

"Oh, I'm sorry. I can imagine it must be hard."

She nodded. "I'm toying with the idea of moving to Massachusetts where my parents and sister live. With Rob gone, I don't see much reason to stay in Sparrow."

"I don't blame you. It's probably a good idea to move closer to your family."

She nodded without looking at me. After a moment of silence, she looked up at me. "I became a school teacher at the insistence of my grandmother. She just knew I would make a great teacher. My parents encouraged me to do whatever I wanted, but I loved my grandmother so much. It seemed she was so full of wisdom, but after I became a teacher, I realized that maybe she didn't know everything. I hate teaching."

"That's a shame. The older I get, the more I can appreciate how important it is to do something you love."

She nodded. "I've been thinking it over for a few years now. It may sound silly, and really, it is, but I have always wanted to own my own business."

"What's silly about that?" I asked and took a sip of my coffee.

She chuckled. "It's the kind of business that I've been thinking about opening that might seem a little silly. A nail salon."

I'll admit, it caught me by surprise. Going from being a teacher to owning a nail salon, was, well, different. "Well, if that's what you feel would make you happy, then why not?"

She shrugged. "I guess it's hard seeing myself telling people I'm quitting a respectable job like teaching to do nails. But it's not the nails I want to do so much as the artwork on the nails. I feel like I can do something unique."

She stuck her hand out so I could see her nails. They looked like they had been hand painted with intricate artwork of a snowy landscape. I had to admit, they were beautiful. "They really are pretty. You did them?"

She smiled and nodded. "It gets a little tricky doing something like that on my right hand."

She showed me her other hand and although it matched the left hand, I could see where it wasn't as detailed. "You do lovely work. If you really want to do it, I say go for it. Forget what other people say."

She beamed at me. "Thanks. I needed to hear that," she said. Then her face clouded over. "I wish Rob had been that supportive. I guess I told you we had some marital troubles. Nothing we wouldn't have worked out, of course. But when I suggested it to him, he freaked out. He refused to give me the money to open a salon in Sparrow."

"Sometimes it's hard for people to get behind another person's dream," I said. I could empathize with Rob. Quitting a teaching job to open something like a nail salon could be taking a big risk. I didn't know how much money a nail salon would bring in, but it might be rough going, at least in the beginning.

"I wish Rob was here. It would have been fun having him by my side as I start this new adventure even if he wasn't completely on board." She sighed. "Can I tell you something?"

I nodded. "Sure."

"I've been thinking things over. I know I mentioned Zack and Rob had troubles, but the more I think about it, the more I really believe that Kyle may have had something to do with Rob's death," she said, leaning in and whispering. "He and Rob had a terrible fight one day. I thought I was going to have to call the police to get them to stop."

"What did they fight over?"

"The inheritance money. Kyle thought it was wrong of Rob to keep all of what he was given even though that was what their parents wanted. I told Rob there was no way he should give his brothers any more than what was designated in the will."

"Money can make people do crazy things," I said. "Did they only fight the one time?"

"Oh no. Kyle called Rob over and over, insisting that giving him more money was the right thing to do. It drove Rob crazy. Finally, he began ignoring his calls, and that was when Kyle came over to the house. It was terrible. Kyle punched Rob. I told him to press charges, but he refused. I was so scared."

"Wow. That's terrible," I said. "I'd be scared, too." I couldn't imagine family fights that became physical.

She nodded. "I'm so glad Kyle won't be coming around anymore. With Rob gone, there's no reason for him to. Having both Kyle and Zack living so close makes moving to Massachusetts more attractive."

I nodded. "Sarah, who is the beneficiary on Rob's bank account?"

"I am. He told me I was. I'm waiting on a copy of the death certificate so I can withdraw the money."

I nodded. I had been fairly sure she would be on the account, but if Rob had put one or both of his brothers on the account as beneficiaries, she might have a surprise in store. And if Kyle were angry enough for things to come to blows, he might have gotten even angrier and drowned Rob in the lake.

Chapter Twelve

"LOOK WHAT I BROUGHT you, George," I said to George Brewster. He was sitting at the front desk at the police station. I was dropping by to visit Cade and I knew I'd hear about it if I came empty-handed.

George's eyes got big. "Wow Rainey, those look so good!"

I smiled. I loved to hear nice things about my baking and cooking. "Lemon poppy seed muffins," I said. "I used fresh lemon juice and grated some of the lemon peel into them." He probably wouldn't appreciate the details of how I made them, but I knew he would appreciate how it made them taste.

"I can smell the lemon from here," he said and slipped a muffin out from beneath the plastic wrap.

"Take another one. I'm taking the rest of these back to the break room and you might not see them again."

"Good idea. Those guys back there will eat them all up before I can get back there to get another one." He took a second muffin and then took a bite of it. He made appreciative sounds while I headed back to Cade's office. "Thanks, Rainey!"

The door was open a few inches, so I knocked and then gently pushed it open. He looked up at me from the paperwork spread out on his desk. "Hey," he said, and then his eyes caught sight of the plate of muffins I held. "Hey, are those for me?"

"Maybe. But I think you can share. I made two dozen," I said and brought them to him.

"Come to Papa," he said and took a muffin from the plate. "They smell great." He took a bite and smiled big.

"I drizzled a thin powered sugar icing on them. Makes them a little tastier," I said and sat down on a visitor's chair in front of his desk. "I'll take the rest of those to the break room before I leave."

"Why? Leave them here. I'll take care of them for you," he said and took another bite.

"I bet you will. What have you found out about the case?"

"He was alive when he went into the water. There was water in his lungs," he said.

"Oh, that's terrible. I hope he was unconscious. What about the phone?"

"Yeah, it's a funny thing about that phone. It didn't belong to Rob," he said. "These are really good." He reached for a second muffin.

"Who did it belong to?"

He looked at me. "Kyle Zumbro."

I gasped. "Wait. Kyle's phone was in the boat? Do you think they went fishing together and then Kyle knocked him in the head and pushed him into the water to drown?" I asked, piecing things together.

"We'll have to see what Kyle has to say about it. I think the tackle box belongs to Zack. It's got more of his fingerprints on it than anyone else's and his fishing license was in it."

I sat back, taking this in. "Wow. Maybe the two of them invited Rob on a fishing trip to do away with him. It would have been easier to kill him with both of them there. They were both practically cut out of their parents' will and they're both bitter about it."

"Could be. That's where I'm headed today. I need to talk to them and see what their story is," he said as he polished off another muffin.

"You better go easy on those. The other guys are going to be mad at you if you eat them all," I said. "And I want to go with you to talk to the Zumbro brothers."

"Finders keepers. I don't care if they do get mad. My girlfriend made them so that makes them mine. And no, you can't go."

"Good. We'd better get moving, I don't have all day."

IT TOOK A LITTLE CONVINCING to get Cade to agree to allow me to go with him, but I have a way with words. I told him he'd never get another muffin as long as he lived if he didn't let me come along.

We dropped by Kyle's house first. There was a big rig truck parked in the wide driveway. The house was on a large lot and there was ample room on either side for the truck to be parked at his house. Kyle was standing beside the cab of the truck and looked up as we pulled into the driveway. Cade parked in front of the truck.

He smiled. "Hey, Rainey, Detective," he said when we got out of the car.

"Hi Kyle," I said, and came around the side of Cade's car.

"Good morning, Kyle," Cade said and glanced at the truck. "No work today?"

"Actually, I was just getting ready to leave. I got a call from dispatch and I've got a load of sand to pick up and deliver on the other side of Boise. What can I help you with?"

"I had a question for you," Cade said, and he pulled the cell phone he had found in Rob's boat out of his coat pocket.

Kyle's eyes got big. The phone was in a plastic evidence bag. "What's that?"

"Your phone," Cade answered.

He looked at Cade. "What do you mean, my phone?"

"It was found in Rob's rowboat. We charged it and called the phone service provider and they said it was registered to you. Didn't you notice that your phone was missing?"

Kyle stared at the phone, then he broke into an uneasy smile. "So that's where it went. I lost it last fall. Rob and I went fishing the weekend before he disappeared and I guess I must have left it behind. Crazy. I never even thought about it being on the rowboat."

Cade gazed at him, a look of uncertainty on his face. "And you didn't ask Rob or his wife if they had seen it? What did you think happened to it?"

He shrugged. "I didn't know where I lost it. I had gone for a hike in the hills before dawn and then went fishing later that morning with Rob. It wasn't until the next day that I realized my phone was gone. I checked the pockets of my windbreaker, but it wasn't there." He nervously shrugged again. "I really thought I lost it out on the hike. It's a cheap phone, I only paid about thirty dollars for it, so I bought another one and transferred the service."

"It really never occurred to you that you might have left it on the boat?" Cade asked.

"No. I don't know why, but I didn't." He shrugged again, his eyes on the phone. Kyle was going to give himself whiplash if he kept the shrugging up.

"Kyle, you had a lot of resentment toward your brother concerning the inheritance money," Cade said. "I think it would be good if we went downtown to talk a little more in depth about that."

"Whoa," Kyle said, putting both hands up, palms facing Cade. "I didn't do anything to my brother. Sure, I was mad that my parents left him most of the money, but I didn't kill him. Wouldn't you be resentful if most of your parents' money went to one of your siblings?"

"Kyle, how much money did Rob inherit from your parents?" I asked him. Everyone talked about the money, but it had never been mentioned exactly how much money it was.

"About three hundred thousand. It's a lot of money, but it's not worth killing over. Besides, if you want to talk to someone, you might talk to Zack. He wanted to get a lawyer and sue Rob for the money."

"A lawyer? Did he hire one?" Cade asked, sounding skeptical.

"He wanted me to pay for half of it, but I didn't have the money. I drive a truck for a living. It's not like it pays peanuts, but I've got a mortgage and three kids. I don't have extra money sitting around. Besides, our parents left the money to Rob. They were in their right minds when they wrote up the will. On what grounds could we sue? I felt like any money spent on a lawyer would be like throwing it away."

He had a point. I didn't know if a judge would allow a lawsuit or not. Didn't people have a right to leave their money to whoever they wanted if they were capable of making the decision?

Cade nodded, thinking this over. "But just because Zack wanted to sue Rob, doesn't mean he'd kill him over it," he pointed out.

"No, but you don't know how mad Zack was. The truth is, when Rob went missing, we thought Sarah had done something to him. I told him we should go to the police, but he wanted to wait and see if Sarah would do something to give herself away. She never did. Then he wanted to wait and see if Rob would come back. We had both started to think that maybe he really did go on an extended fishing trip, but when that never happened, I had to wonder why Zack was okay with continuing to wait. Made me wonder if he had a reason to keep the police out of it."

Cade narrowed his eyes at Kyle. "Why don't we go downtown and talk this through," he suggested. "There are too many holes in your story."

"Aw, come on, don't do that to me. I've got to get to work. I've got three kids to feed. My wife left us last year and I'm their only support. I promise to come and see you when I'm done, but let me work this job," he pleaded. "It's not like I'm going to take off with three kids and a big rig."

Cade hesitated a moment, then said, "I want to see you at the station as soon as you finish up today. If I have to come looking for you, you'll regret it."

He nodded. "You got it. I promise."

We headed back to Cade's car and got in. Cade backed the car out of the driveway so Kyle could leave.

"What do you think?" I asked as we watched Kyle climb into the cab of his truck.

"Lots of holes. I don't know. We'll see what he has to say when I talk to him tonight."

"That was nice of you to let him go to work," I said.

"He's right. It's not like he's going to run with the kids. He's got ties to the community. Besides, I'm not ready to arrest him, so it would be pretty mean-spirited of me to keep him from working."

"That's true. Let's go talk to Zack." Both Kyle and Zack had pointed fingers at one another. It didn't give me a warm fuzzy feeling about their family dynamics.

He glanced at me. "Yes ma'am."

Chapter Thirteen

WHEN WE GOT TO THE feed store, there were three customers inside. One was buying three sacks of chicken feed, the second was looking over the saddles, and the last had a little boy in tow who was obsessed with the guinea pigs.

"Well?" I said to Cade. Zack's assistant was helping the elderly man that had bought the chicken feed, and Zack was talking to the man in the cowboy hat that was looking at the saddles.

"Well, I guess we should wait a few minutes," Cade said. He looked over the store and inhaled deeply. The fire was crackling and the store smelled of leather and feed above the scent of burning wood. "I think this is the first time I've been in a feed store."

"Seriously? Like, ever?" I asked him.

He nodded. "I've never been an animal person. What about you?"

"I'll admit until last week, I had never been in this one, but when I was a kid, my dad took me to one in Boise in search of a blond guinea pig. But there's something you should know about this place."

"What's that?" he asked, turning to me.

"They sell fishing equipment."

"What?" he said, looking around. "Where?"

"Walk this way," I said and led him to the last aisle. Zack waved at me as I passed.

"How did I not know this?" he asked, looking over the fishing rods.

"I don't know. I'm kind of surprised, to tell you the truth. And they've got bait. Stinky marshmallows, worms, and ew, live crickets. Gross."

He picked up a fishing rod and tried it out. "I usually get my equipment at sporting good stores or online. I've been missing out."

I sighed. "You poor thing."

"They don't have the really specialized equipment, but this is a decent selection of mid-grade lures, sinkers, and reels. Next time we go fishing, I'm bringing crickets for you."

I laughed. "Bring what you want, but no way am I going near crickets."

When the customer that had been looking over the saddles left, Zack headed in our direction. "Hey, Rainey," he said hesitantly.

"Yup, you got it right," I said and smiled.

He smiled at being able to tell me apart from my sister. Or maybe it was because I was with Cade. He looked at him and nodded. "Detective."

"Good morning, Zack, can we have a few minutes of your time?" Cade asked.

Zack stopped smiling. "Sure. We can go into my office if you'd like. Brian can take care of customers by himself for a few minutes."

We followed Zack to the back of the store and down a hallway that led to a large room. I glanced around. The room had a small desk against one wall and a table in the middle of it. Zack's office also served as a break room. There was a microwave and a coffee pot on a counter and a refrigerator in the corner.

"Why don't we sit at the table? Can I get either of you some coffee? It's plain old joe, but it's good and hot," he offered.

"No, thanks," Cade said. "I'm fine."

"I just had a cup," I said.

"Okay, well then, I think I'll pour myself a cup," he said and went to the coffee pot on the counter, and took a cup from the cupboard above it. He suddenly seemed nervous.

When he finished pouring a cup of coffee, he came over and sat across from us. I caught the slight tremble of his hands as he held the coffee cup between them.

"Zack, I don't want to take up a lot of your time, but can you show me your fishing license?" Cade asked.

Zack's brow furrowed. "Fishing license?" he asked, puzzled.

Cade nodded. "Please."

"I think it's at home. Why would you want to see my fishing license?"

Cade pulled the license from his pocket and tossed it on the table. "I don't think it's at home."

I was surprised. Cade suddenly sounded cold. It reminded me of when I first met him and he had questioned me about another murder. Cade could become all business at the drop of a hat.

Zack's eyes were on the fishing license. Then he looked up at Cade. "To be honest, I haven't gone fishing in months. I just assumed it was at home. Where did you find it?"

"It was in a tackle box that was on Rob's boat. Care to tell me how it got there?"

Zack's face drained of color. "I went fishing with him last summer or early fall, right before he disappeared. I forget exactly what day it was. There was a fish and game warden that came by and asked for our licenses right as we were getting into the boat. I guess I must not have put it back into my wallet after he took a look at it. Why?"

Cade shrugged slowly. "What about the lawyer you were going to hire to try to get your parents' money back from Rob? Was it too expensive to hire one? Maybe it was easier to knock him off. I'm not saying it was planned, but maybe you saw your chance while out on the boat fishing and you hit him over the head and pushed him into the water on a whim."

Zack's eyes got big. He opened his mouth to say something and then shut it. He looked at me, pleading with his eyes. I was as shocked at this change in Cade as Zack was. I couldn't offer him any help.

"No!" he finally said. "I never harmed Rob. Sure, I thought about getting a lawyer. It was wrong what my parents did, but no way would I kill him over it! And you can ask the game warden. Charlie Cooper. I bet he'll remember asking us for our licenses. He stood there and talked to us a good fifteen minutes about fishing. Ask him!"

Cade considered this. "You sure he'll vouch for you?"

He nodded furiously. "I've got a family. I wouldn't jeopardize their future by killing my brother. And besides, he was my brother! As mad as I was that he wouldn't share the money, I would never kill him. You've got to believe me."

"I hope for your sake that you're telling the truth," Cade warned.

"I am. I really am." Zack looked at me again, then back at Cade.

Cade stared him down another minute, then looked at me. "Did you have any questions for him?"

I was so stunned he asked that I couldn't come up with a thing.

He turned back to Zack. "I'll be around with more questions after I check with Charlie Cooper. If there's something you can think of that will help catch the killer, I expect you to tell me."

He nodded. "I do have something. I think Rob's wife killed him. When we were fishing, Rob complained about her. He said she was riding him hard about giving her some money to open a nail salon. Rob thought it was ridiculous, and he told her it would be over his dead body. He said that she said she didn't have a problem with that and he better watch his back. You should talk to her." He nodded his head again for emphasis.

"He said she told him to watch his back?" Cade asked.

He nodded again. "Yeah. He laughed it off. I told him he better be careful. He thought it was ridiculous for her to give up a teaching career to do nails. And everyone knows how tight Sarah is with money. She's greedy. Ever since his body was found, I can't get that conversation out of my mind. I think Sarah did it." He licked his lips and glanced at me again.

"I'll definitely check into it," Cade said. "Anything else?"

He shook his head. "No, but I'm telling you, if anyone did it, it was Sarah. I've never trusted her. Ask Kyle. He'll tell you what she's like."

"Great. Thanks for the info," Cade said and got to his feet and without another word, headed for the door without waiting for me. I got up and followed him out of the room without saying anything else to Zack.

"I can't believe you did that!" I said when we were back in his car. "You play 'bad cop' really well!"

He shrugged. "It's a gift. You weren't very helpful in there. You need to at least try to be the good cop."

I chuckled. "Yeah, I'll work on that. Are we going to talk to Sarah?"

"She's at work right now. I don't want to scare a bunch of little kids."

"You're not that bad, then. Can I come with you when you do talk to her?"

"No. I shouldn't have allowed you to come along today. Now, I've got to get back to work. I'll drop you off at home."

"That was genius when you turned and asked me if I had anything," I said and chuckled again. I hated to be mean to Zack. He seemed like a nice guy. But if he had actually killed his brother, I wouldn't feel bad about Cade coming down so hard on him.

He smiled and started the car.

Chapter Fourteen

IT WAS TWO DAYS LATER when Cade showed up at my front door in his fluorescent orange overalls and a smile on his face.

"What are you doing here?" I asked when I answered the door. I looked him up and down. I knew what that outfit meant, and it didn't bring a smile to my face.

He grinned. "That's no way to greet the man of your dreams."

I narrowed my eyes at him. "It is when that man shows up in that getup. I know what that means."

"Indeed, you do. Let's go fishing. You owe me a fried fish dinner," he said and followed me into the house.

"I told you, I don't want fish that have nibbled on a dead man," I said, picking up my coffee cup and taking a sip. It had been two weeks since we had found Rob Zumbro in the lake and I wasn't ready to go back.

"You're so hostile today," he said with a grin. "It's been long enough for the fish to get the dead guy out of their systems. They'll be nice and fresh and ready to be caught." He looked at the cup in my hand. "Coffee?"

"Come on," I said and headed to the kitchen. I got him a cup out of the cupboard and poured him some coffee.

"Thanks. If I remember right, today is your day off. Now, if you'll go with me, we might run into the game warden and see if Zack's story pans out." He took a sip of his coffee and grimaced. "Needs sugar and cream." He went to my refrigerator and helped himself.

I groaned. "Well, if it will help the case, maybe I can make the sacrifice," I said. "I'll change into warmer clothes."

"That's the spirit," he called after me. "Sometimes sacrifices have to be made in the line of duty."

I groaned again. That man was going to be the death of me one day.

I WAS THANKFUL THAT the day was bright and clear and the wind was almost nonexistent. It helped to keep the cold at bay. I lugged the folding chairs from the trunk of Cade's car toward the lakeshore. I really didn't want to step out onto that ice, but I knew it would be pointless to argue with him.

"What a wonderful day," he almost sang. "I can just imagine all the tasty fish we're going to catch."

"I don't want to go out on the ice," I whined. I was suddenly having flashbacks of that red jacket floating beneath the ice and I didn't like it.

"Come on now, we have to be on the ice to go ice fishing," he said and pulled the tackle box out of the trunk. "Otherwise it's just called fishing."

"I thought we were looking for the game warden. How is he going to find us if we're out on the ice?" I asked as we lugged the equipment to the bank.

"He'll simply walk out onto the ice and ask us for our licenses," Cade said.

"But couldn't we just call the game warden and ask him if he talked to Zack and Rob last fall?"

He chuckled. "You sure are the reluctant fisherwoman, aren't you? Where's your spirit? Let's catch some fish!"

"You don't have to be so enthusiastic," I grumbled. "Did you bring the thermos of coffee? Because I think I'm going to need it." I had put on two layers beneath my jeans and sweatshirt and my feet were protected with two pairs of wool socks. I wore a heavy coat, wool beanie, and a thick scarf wrapped around my neck. All in all, I wasn't nearly as cold as I was the first time we went fishing. At least there was that.

"Wait right here," he said when we got to the ice and he trotted back to the car, taking out the ice chest. I didn't think we needed one. It was cold enough without it, but I had packed a lunch of ham and cheese sandwiches, half an apple pie, and macaroni salad. If nothing else, the ice chest would protect the food from getting anything in it as we lugged it from the car.

Cade walked out onto the ice and I reluctantly followed him. A hawk flew low overhead, and I reflexively ducked as its shadow passed over us. "Wow," I said. I couldn't help but look at the ice as we walked. I didn't feel any more secure on it than I had the last time. And as much as I would rather not look at it, I couldn't help myself. I still couldn't get over being able to see the fish beneath the ice.

"Relax," he said and laid the equipment down and then headed back for the rest.

"Relax," I mimicked. "You'll say relax if we find another body."

"What's that? I can't hear you!" he called over his shoulder.

I snorted and set up the chairs. If he wasn't careful, I was going to eat all the apple pie and not share with him.

"We don't have to stay all day, do we?" I asked, trying to keep the whine out of my voice.

Cade returned with the auger. "Depends on how fast we catch fish. You better get going," he said as he began drilling a hole into the ice.

I sat in my chair and waited for him to finish and then bait my hook. A pickup drove slowly by on the shore and parked near his car.

"Is that the game warden?" I asked as I squinted my eyes at the emblem on the door of the truck.

"It is," he said. We waited until he got out and made his way over to us.

"Detective Starkey?" he asked.

Cade nodded and shook hands with him.

"Hi Charlie," I said. I had known Charlie since the second grade when his family had moved to Sparrow from California. He had once been ridiculed for several weeks when he brought an avocado and bean sprout sandwich to school in his lunch box.

"Hi, Rainey," he said. "Doing a little fishing?"

I shrugged. "I guess you could call it that."

He chuckled and turned back to Cade. "I take it she's not a fan."

Cade shook his head. "Not even a little bit."

He nodded. "I got your message this morning. I thought I'd come out here and say hello and introduce myself."

"Wait, you called him? You couldn't just ask him what you needed to know?" I said to Cade.

"I told you. We need fish," he said, then turned back to Charlie. "I know this is a shot in the dark, but do you happen to remember running into Rob and Zack Zumbro late last summer? Zack said you checked their fishing licenses."

Charlie thought about it. "I know I checked them, but I couldn't tell you exactly when it was. It most likely was late summer. I heard they pulled Rob from this lake a couple of weeks ago. It's a shame."

Cade nodded. "It is. We're hoping to make an arrest soon."

"You don't think Zack had something to do with it, do you? Is that why you're asking about the licenses?"

"It's early in the investigation yet, and I'm just checking out stories. I found Zack's fishing license in Rob's rowboat. I just wondered about it," Cade said.

"Well, I'd hate to think he might have had something to do with his brother's death. The Zumbros are good people. Their father used to come out and fish regularly. It was a tragedy that he and his wife died like they did. I'd seen him a week before they had the accident."

"Did he say anything of interest?" Cade asked.

Charlie thought about it a moment. "We talked about a lot of different things. He was a pleasant guy to talk to. I do remember that he asked if I knew a good lawyer. The one he'd used previously had retired."

"What did he need a lawyer for?" Cade asked.

"Said he wanted to change his will. He said he'd been thinking about things and he'd made a mistake. He said he wanted to make things right."

My stomach dropped. Had the senior Zumbro changed his mind about his will and decided to divide the money evenly between his sons?

"Really?" Cade asked. "Did he elaborate?"

"Nah, he just said he'd had a change of heart about something. I try not to pry into folks' business, but he seemed kind of regretful," he said. "Makes me wonder if he somehow knew his time was coming, and that was why he wanted to change it. Some people have a sense of those kinds of things. I hope he got his business taken care of before it was too late."

Cade nodded. "I hope so. Makes you think about things when people die suddenly, doesn't it?"

"You better believe it. It makes me appreciate my own family that much more," Charlie said. "I hear the trout are biting. I saw Jim Edwards pull one out of this lake last week that must have weighed fifteen pounds."

"Trout are good eating," Cade said, shooting me a look.

I rolled my eyes. "You can get perfectly good trout at the grocery store," I reminded him.

They both laughed at me. Let them laugh it up, I thought. If we pull another body out of this lake, my fishing days are over.

"Well, it was good meeting you, Cade," Charlie said. "I've got to make the rounds now."

"Good meeting you, too," Cade said.

"See you later, Rainey," he said and carefully headed back to his truck.

I looked at Cade. "Did you hear that? Mr. Zumbro wanted to make a change to his will!"

"Sounds like he didn't get it done," Cade said.

"Kind of sad. If he had made the change, maybe Rob would still be alive if it was one of his brothers that killed him," I said and handed him my fishing pole so he could put bait on the hook.

"That's something to think about," he said. "Stinky marshmallows?"

"My favorite," I said without enthusiasm.

If it was true that Mr. Zumbro had intended to change the will, it made things sadder. Rob might not have been entitled to as much money as he had ended up with and maybe he'd be alive now. I had had time to think about things and if my mother left all her money to me, I would definitely give Stormy half of it. Money wasn't worth splitting families up over.

Chapter Fifteen

I SQUINTED MY EYES as I looked over the recipe I had just typed up. It seemed that something was missing, but I wasn't sure what. I picked up the piece of paper I had jotted down the ingredients on. It was stained with butter and floury smudges. The baklava I had made for Cade last month had been delicious. Although not exactly an American recipe, it was still a tradition in many American homes at Christmas time and I thought I could get away with including it. The problem was, I had written down the amounts of flour and sugar, and then crossed them out and re-wrote them next to it. I had made the recipe four times, not quite satisfied with the results, and changed the amounts of nearly every ingredient each time. It would have been easier to start with a known recipe and make tweaks, but when I get something in my head, I've got to try it out. So went the baklava recipe.

Maggie lay at my feet, snoring lightly. I ran a toe along her ribs and she rewarded me with a thump of her tail against the floor. The doorbell rang, and she raised her head, all attention on the office doorway now.

"Let's see who that is," I said and got up.

Maggie padded after me as I headed to the front door. "Hey, Stormy, Mom," I said when I opened the door. "What are you two doing?" The snow was falling softly, making my front yard look like a winter wonderland.

"We wanted to see what you were up to," Stormy said.

"I'm working on the cookbook," I said and led the way into the kitchen. "Coffee anyone?"

"I'd love some coffee," Mom said. "Maggie, you get prettier every time I see you." She reached down and scratched Maggie's ear.

"I think she's been wondering where you've been," I told her as I went to the coffee pot and measured out ground coffee.

"Well I missed her, too," Mom said in baby-talk she reserved for animals and small children.

"Mom has something to show you," Stormy announced.

I turned to look at her, the water pitcher poised to pour into the coffee pot. "You do?"

Mom shrugged. "I was digging in an old box and I found something."

I turned back to the coffee pot and finished filling it with water. "What's that?" I poured the water into the machine and turned it on.

"This," she said, holding out a yellowed envelope.

"What's that?" I asked, taking it from her. Her name and our old address were printed neatly on the front in large block letters and numbers.

"A letter from Barron Zumbro. I didn't realize I still had it, but when you mentioned him the other day, I got to thinking about him and remembered he had sent me a letter. I swore I didn't have it anymore, but I thought I'd check in an old box that I kept letters and cards in. And there it was."

"Can I read it?" I asked.

She nodded. "Sure, why not? There's really nothing personal in it, I just thought it was interesting since you brought his name up. I had forgotten all about him, to tell you the truth. I'm surprised he even remembered you."

I nodded and opened the envelope, taking out the yellowed pages. The coffee pot was perking and the smell of freshly brewed coffee filled the kitchen. I sank down into a chair and leaned on the table, unfolding the letter. There were two pages, each filled with the same large block letters that were on the envelope. Apparently Barron wasn't much on cursive.

Dearest Mary Ann,

I know this letter may surprise you, but I couldn't keep myself from writing. I completely understand why you don't want to see me again, but I wanted to ask you to give me one more chance. No, I wanted to beg you to give me one more chance. I know there are rumors going around this town about me, but you have to understand that most of them aren't true. I suppose there are some things that are true, but you have to believe me when I say that I've repented for my misdeeds, and I've changed.

Mary Ann, I can give you a good life. I'm a changed man and I can be a good step-father to your daughters. One that you would be proud of. I can promise you that. Will you just give me one more chance?

I looked up at Mom. She was twiddling her thumbs, and she shrugged. "I don't know how I forgot about that letter."

"I don't either," I said and continued reading. The rest of the letter detailed what he thought would be a happy life with her and me and Stormy. It could have been seen as sweet, but for some reason, it felt kind of icky. "He sounded desperate."

"It's weird," Stormy said. "He didn't even know her that well and he was practically proposing."

I nodded. "It is weird." Barron seemed to make an attachment to my mother, and by extension, to Stormy and me. I didn't know whether to feel sorry for him or not, but it made me uncomfortable.

"I just thought I'd bring it by for you to read. I didn't call it off with him for any reason other than I missed your father. I explained that to him, but he thought he could change my mind," Mom said.

"It seems like he thought you didn't want to go out with him because of rumors you may have heard about him," I said.

Mom was quiet a moment. "I remember a conversation I had with him. He said his parents had cut him out of their will. He was angry. They were going to leave all their money to his brother."

"That sounds familiar," I said. "Why did they cut him out of the will?"

"Because he had shamed them. His drug and alcohol use cost him a chance at qualifying for the Olympics and his parents couldn't seem to forgive him."

"Seems kind of harsh," I said. "His parents were still alive at the time he wrote this letter?"

She nodded. "I guess they had a small fortune, according to Barron. They had scrimped and saved all their lives. Their businesses didn't seem to work out, but somehow they had put away half a million dollars and they were leaving all of it to his brother."

"He told you how much money it was?" I asked and got up to pour coffee. I got the sugar and the cream from the refrigerator and set them on the table.

"Yes, he told me it was a half-million. I wondered if it was true because he seemed so intently focused on the number. It made me feel like he might be exaggerating the amount. Like maybe he didn't really know how much there was and he was just guessing."

"Is that what freaked you out?" I asked her and got three cups from the cupboard. Kyle said Rob inherited three hundred thousand, but it easily could have originally been a half-million.

"I wasn't freaked out. It was just weird. I think I compared him to your father, and I realized he couldn't measure up. But then, no man ever could. Your father was such a wonderful man. I thought that if it was meant to be, then I should feel more comfortable. Otherwise, I'd stay by myself. I had you girls to think about. Plus Natalie was a toddler, and I didn't want someone I didn't feel completely comfortable about around her."

I felt bad for Mom. I hadn't thought much about her dating. She hadn't had much interest, and I thought she was happy. But maybe she was lonely and would have appreciated some companionship.

"After reading that letter, I'm glad you went with your instincts," I said and poured the coffee into the cups. "He seemed desperate. Bill from the newspaper told me he didn't seem to have much direction in life after he got kicked out of college. Honestly, he could have gone to another college and made something of himself. It stinks that he couldn't get himself together before it was too late to compete at the Olympics, but still, he could have had a career," I said and sat down again. "How has he supported himself all these years?"

She shrugged. "At the time we went out, he worked as an usher at the movie theater."

"What does Cade say about the murder?" Stormy asked, pouring cream into her coffee.

Maggie lay down at Mom's feet and groaned, resting her chin on her shoe.

"He's still looking into it. I think he may make an arrest soon, but that's between the three of us. Rob's brothers are kind of sketchy."

"Oh," Stormy said sadly. "I hate to hear that. They're both really nice guys. Or at least I thought they were."

"Well, I'm not saying he will definitely arrest them. They just seem suspicious," I said.

"Did he say why specifically?" she asked. "He has to have something solid before he arrests anyone, right?"

I regretted telling her Cade might make an arrest soon and that the two brothers seemed sketchy. I had momentarily forgotten that she was friendly with them. "He keeps most things to himself. Sorry, I shouldn't have said anything. I don't know for sure that he will arrest either of them."

She nodded. "I won't say anything to anyone, and maybe Cade will change his mind."

I sighed. I needed to learn to keep my mouth shut. The letter from Barron was interesting, and it gave me insight into his personality. It also gave me a little insight into my mother's life, but I was glad she had chosen to break it off with him. I suspected he might have been interested in her because she owned her own business and needed someone to support him.

Chapter sixteen

"WHAT'S THAT?" SAM ASKED, peering into the plastic bowl that I held.

"The dry ingredients of my new herb battered coating for fried fish. I thought of it in the middle of the night. Cade is determined to make me go fishing again, so I figured I may as well cooperate and whip up a tasty flavorful coating for fish that will fry up nice and crisp."

"Oh," he said, sounding disappointed. "I was thinking you might bring us cupcakes."

"Why would I bring in cupcakes?" I couldn't remember promising cupcakes, but maybe I had forgotten.

He shrugged. "I'm in the mood for them and I was hoping you could read my mind." He went back to the grill and scrubbed it with a wire brush. We had a lull between the breakfast and lunch customers and Sam was using that time to clean the grill.

"I can't read minds," I said and went to the refrigerator and peered in. "So, no enthusiasm for fried fish?"

"Sounds good. We just got some trout fillets in. You could try it on that," he said.

"Trout?" Ron white, our dishwasher asked, turning toward me. "I like trout."

"That's what I'm talking about," I said. "Enthusiasm for the fish." I pulled out two eggs and a gallon of milk and set them on the counter. Then I took a shallow bowl from the cupboard and cracked the eggs into it, and then I added milk and whisked them together.

"Fish is good," Sam said. He still wasn't showing much enthusiasm, but he would change his tune when he tasted the fish. I was also working on a recipe for hushpuppies. Cade would drool over them when I made them for him.

I heard a heavy sigh from behind me and I didn't even need to turn around to see who it was. Georgia Johnson had arrived.

"What do you want, Georgia?" I asked without looking at her. I went to the refrigerator and pulled out some fresh chives and two garlic cloves and took them back to where I was working.

"Why are you always back here when you should be out front? Working?" she growled. Georgia and I had a history, and it wasn't a good one. She didn't like me for some reason, not that I understood what that reason was. She was keeping it a secret, even from me.

"Because business is slow. There's only one customer out there, unless some just walked in." I pulled out a cutting board and began finely chopping the chives.

"That's just it. You'll never know because you're back here instead of up front waiting on customers," she said. "You've probably forgotten that that's your job, so let me remind you—that's your job."

I glanced at her. She had her bleached blond hair piled up on her head and her hands on her hips, waiting for me to respond. I decided to ignore her. I never got anywhere when I tried talking to her like an adult.

"Georgia?" Sam said.

"What?" she answered without taking her eyes off me.

"Are there customers out there that Rainey needs to see to?"

"No, but that's not the point," she huffed.

"Rainey is busy cooking us some lunch. Why don't you go out front and wait for customers, and she'll make a tasty meal for us," Sam said. He was being too kind. She didn't appreciate that he was a good boss and anyone else would have told her where to get off.

She sighed again.

Let the drama begin.

"I heard there was a dead body found in the lake," she suddenly said, changing her tone.

I glanced at her. The attitude was gone and now she seemed more relaxed. I nodded. "Yes, there was a body found out there."

"That's too bad. I heard a person could die in a lake and not be found for years. If the lake water stays cold enough, the body can be perfectly preserved, even after twenty years. Unless, of course, the fish snack on it," she said and then chuckled.

"I don't know about that. Twenty years seems like a long time," I said, wishing she would just go and tend to the one customer we had.

"When I was in fifth grade, Yvonne Ellis's dad disappeared in the lake. They never found him. Everyone would ask her if her dad was sleeping with the fishes. It was a riot."

I had forgotten about that. It had been rumored that Yvonne's dad actually had a girlfriend that he ran off with. Georgia was ten years younger than I was, and my mother had told me the news after I had moved to New York.

"That's a shame. Kids can be cruel. I'm sure it wasn't much of a riot for Yvonne," I said, hoping she'd get the hint that I didn't want to talk to her. I went to the refrigerator and pulled out the trout Sam had offered.

"I bet his wife killed him," Georgia said when I didn't say anything more.

"Yvonne's mom?" I asked, confused.

She snorted. "No. The guy they just found."

"Why do you think that?" Ron asked, rinsing a stockpot beneath the faucet.

"Because she was at the bar one night after she and her husband had a big fight. Can you imagine that? A second grade teacher at the bar?" she said and snorted again. "That would go over real well with the kids' parents if they knew. Anyway, she was mad at him and she said he was a tightwad and wouldn't give her any of the money his parents left him. She thought she deserved some of it for putting up with him."

I glanced at her. I didn't want to show interest in what she was saying because that would keep her in the kitchen longer. I had given up on making nice with her. She was rarely anything but hateful to me.

"Why does that make you think she killed her husband?" Sam asked, relieving me of the need to ask.

"Because she said she was going to get her hands on that money, one way or another. Me and a couple other ladies had gathered around her and she was really tying one on. She said it might take her a little time, but she'd do it. She'd have that money to open a nail salon."

I turned to look at her. I couldn't help it; I needed to know. "Did she say how she intended to get the money?" I asked.

"Nope. But she said one day in the not too distant future, she'd be a rich woman. I thought she was just going to find a way to get the money out of the bank, like order a second ATM card or something. But no, she killed him instead. Not a bad idea if she had life insurance on him too. Something like that would really pay off."

It was all I could do to keep from staring openmouthed at her. Sarah had said she was using the insurance money she was going to collect from Rob's death to start her business. And a second ATM card? Cade needed to get the videos from the bank as soon as he could.

"That's a real shame," Sam said and glanced at me.

I stared back at him. "I can't imagine someone killing over money," I said and went back to mixing the batter for the fish. "What a terrible person that would be, if that's what happened."

"Money is the root of all evil," Ron said and began rinsing the sink out.

"The love of money is the root of all evil," I corrected. "That's from the bible and I have to say, I think I just might believe it."

He chuckled. "I think I might believe it, too."

I took down a plate from the cupboard, thinking things over. Maybe Sarah hadn't ordered a new ATM card. Maybe Rob's wallet hadn't been lost at the bottom of the lake at all and she had the wallet and his card. It would be easy to pull that money out of the ATM if she had his wallet. If she drove around to different ATMs, she might make it look like Rob was indeed traveling around Idaho and nearby states, enjoying an extended fishing trip. But she had to know that all banks have cameras. Unless a camera happened to go on the fritz, there would be footage. And even if one camera wasn't working, she had said there had been multiple withdrawals from different banks. Several of those cameras had to have caught whoever was withdrawing money from Rob's account.

But that made me wonder. Had she found a way to fool the cameras? Would she know how to block the cameras? Was it even possible? I didn't think so, but I didn't know enough about bank cameras to know for sure. That left a disguise. Could she have covered her face somehow? But Rob was tall, and she wasn't anywhere near that tall, so it would be obvious it wasn't him. Unless she had teamed up with a man that had a similar build and resembled Rob. And that could be either one of his brothers.

Chapter Seventeen

"OKAY MAGGIE, YOU'RE my secret weapon," I whispered as I let her out of the car. I hooked the leash to her collar, and we headed into the feed store. The sky was gray and there was a chilly breeze blowing, so I hurried as quickly as I dared on the icy sidewalk.

Maggie was all eyes and ears as we headed inside the feed store. "Be a good girl," I said, putting one hand on her shoulders as she got wind of the guinea pigs. Her ears went forward and her nose twitched and I tightened my grip on the leash.

Zack's assistant looked up from the case of horse brushes he was unpacking in the nearest aisle. "That's a nice looking hound dog there," he said. "I bet she'd tree a bear in no time."

"Thanks. I think she's pretty too, but I have no idea about treeing bears. She's a city dog," I said and allowed Maggie to go to him. "She loves people."

"I see that," he said as Maggie went to him, wagging her tail. Her nose twitched back and forth and her body got into the action as she tried to control her excitement at getting to meet someone new. He let her sniff his hand, then he bent over and rubbed her head with both hands. "What a good girl."

"Careful or she'll jump on you," I warned and moved closer to Maggie.

"That's okay. I've got three dogs and they're all big ones. I can take it," he said as he rubbed her back. When he straightened up, Maggie took that as an invitation to give him love, and stood on her back feet, placing both paws on his chest.

I grinned. "I told you. She loves people. I thought I'd bring her in so she can pick out her own food," I said and pulled Maggie off of him.

He laughed. "That may not be a good idea. She'll pick treats instead of food."

"I didn't think of that," I said. He was probably right. Maggie loved her treats.

Zack walked around the corner to see what the fuss was in our aisle and stopped when he saw me. His mouth pressed together, then he saw Maggie and smiled. "That's quite the dog you have there," he said stiffly. I knew Maggie's charms would work on him.

"Thank you," I said. "She saved my life a few months back. I couldn't leave her behind at the shelter after that."

"How did she do that?" he asked as Maggie went to check him out.

"A murderer tried to make me his second victim, and she stopped him," I said.

He narrowed his eyes at me. "Do you make a habit of chasing down murderers?"

I wasn't sure what to say to that. "It's not a habit," I said feeling defensive. "Look, I just thought I'd stop in and pick up some dog food." I knew he wouldn't appreciate me coming around after what had happened when Cade and I were here the last time. That's why I needed Maggie. She'd smooth things over.

"Let me show you where that is," he said and led the way down another aisle.

Maggie and I followed, but then Maggie caught the scent of the guinea pigs again and jerked the leash in that direction. "Hold on Maggie," I said. She whimpered and pulled on the leash. I was going to have to get her some obedience lessons if I intended to bring her out in public regularly.

"Hunting dogs got to hunt," Zack said, over his shoulder. "Do you need help?"

"I think I got it," I said, but I may have sounded more confident that I felt. After a minute or so I got Maggie under control and led her back in the direction of the dog food. I smiled at Zack, but he didn't respond with a smile of his own as I'd hoped.

"We've got all kinds of dog food. There are some grain free options, or there's some regular dog food. How old is she?"

"They said she was about two years old when I got her at the shelter."

He nodded. "The grain free options are good. This one is very good. I feed my own dogs this one." He picked up a large bag with the picture of a bird dog on it. "It's good for working dogs. Are you going to hunt her?"

I shook my head. "No, I don't think that will ever happen. I'm an indoors kind of person. Look Maggie, this food is for hunting dogs, I bet you'll like it," I said, laying a hand on her head.

Zack was all business, avoiding making eye contact with me. "Is this the one you want?"

"It looks good to me. I think I want to pick up some treats, too," I said. Zack was tall, like his brothers. Cade had said Rob was about 6'3" and I'd guess Zack was a little taller. If he wore a baseball hat and kept his head down, it was possible the ATM camera wouldn't be able to get a clear picture of him. It made me wonder.

He picked up the bag of food and led me further down the aisle and stopped in front of a display. "We've got pig ears, rawhide, and all kinds of dog cookies."

"Ew, pig ears? Real pig ears? Gross."

"Don't knock them until you try them," he said without smiling.

Maggie's nose started twitching, and she pulled on the leash so she could inspect the dog treats.

"Now, Maggie, you can't have those. We have to pay for them," I warned her.

"Here Maggie, here's a cookie," he said, taking one out of a jar and tossing it to her. Maggie made short work of it and looked at him expectantly. He smiled and tossed her a second cookie. It was impossible for him to be angry with Maggie around. I knew my plan would work.

"Zack, I wanted to apologize if Cade came on too strong the other day," I said. It might not have been what Cade would have wanted me to say, but I was hoping to get on Zack's good side so he might help me out and tell me more about what he might know about what happened to his brother.

He snorted. "I did not kill my brother. It's ridiculous if anyone thinks there's even a possibility of that happening. I don't know why he thinks I might have done it. Who told him I did? Did someone say I did it? Is that why he's looking at me?"

"You know, Zack, I really don't know." It was a lie, but I couldn't tell him his own brother had pointed a finger at him. There was enough trouble in this family. "I'm sure Cade needs to check out all possible leads." That was true. Just because Charlie Cooper had confirmed he had checked his and Rob's fishing licenses, didn't mean a thing. Charlie couldn't remember exactly when that was. And even if he had done it the day Zack said he had, he still could have killed Rob later that day.

He gritted his teeth. "I'm telling you, you need to check out Sarah's story. Who sits by while their husband is gone for months without reporting him? And she had insurance money on him! It's a waste of time to look at anyone other than her."

My idea of talking to Zack and trying to get more information out of him was backfiring. His face was turning red, and he was becoming agitated. I had had visions of him encouraging me to keep looking for his brother's killer and maybe giving me more clues, but it was now clear that that wasn't going to happen.

"Listen, Zack, I totally get where you're coming from. I feel terrible that Rob died. But I think it's just procedure for the police to investigate people that are the closest to the victim. They always think that when someone goes missing or is murdered, it's probably the closest family members, right? I know Cade is doing everything he can to find Rob's killer and I just know he's going to get a major lead any day now."

"What makes you say that?" he asked, jutting his chin out defensively.

I stopped and looked at him. "Well, okay. Maybe I don't know that for sure. I mean, I don't know what all of his leads are. He doesn't always share that kind of information with me. But I know Cade, and he's determined to find the killer." I was getting in deep and I needed a way out. I reached down and rubbed Maggie's head.

He thought this over. "Okay, fine. As long as he's looking into Sarah's story, I guess there isn't much else I can do. I just don't want her to be overlooked," he relented. "I know she had to have something to do with his death to be able to sit there for months without worrying about him being gone."

I nodded. "You can bet Cade is looking into every clue as well as everyone that was close to Rob."

"Did he talk to Charlie Cooper? Did he verify what I said?"

I hesitated. I didn't want to give too much away, but I figured if he ran into Charlie, he'd ask him anyway. I nodded. "He sure did. Said he saw you and Rob getting ready to go out on the water." I smiled.

He nodded. "Good. As long as Cade knows I wasn't lying about the fishing license. Let me take this bag of dog food to the front counter for you. It's heavy. Brian will help you out to your car with it," he said and headed to the front.

I sighed and led Maggie after him. A chirping sound came from another aisle and Maggie was off and running. I barely managed to keep hold of her leash as she dragged me along behind her. "Stop, Maggie!" I called.

I heard laughter from the direction of the front counter. Great. I could use some help instead of laughter. "Come on, Maggie."

Maggie scented out the chirping sound in less than a minute. It was a cage full of tiny finches. She bayed at them, causing them to flee to the furthest side of their cage. I put a hand on her muzzle to quiet her down. "Hush, you're scaring them," I said. "The poor little things." Several of the birds flew to higher perches where they turned their heads to get a better look at who had disturbed their day.

"Sorry little guys," I apologized and had to half-drag Maggie back to the front counter.

Zack and Brian were still chuckling when I got there. I stopped and narrowed my eyes at them. "I'm glad this is so amusing."

Zack shrugged. "You might reconsider bringing a hunting dog into a place where there are small animals. It's instinct for her to hunt them down. Good thing they're in cages or we'd have a disaster on our hands."

I bit my lower lip. "Sorry. It didn't occur to me." Then I shrugged. The little animals had survived our visit unharmed and Maggie got to go on a short trip.

And at least Zack had lightened up. He seemed like a nice guy and I really hoped he hadn't killed his brother. It would make me feel even worse about the fact that Rob had been murdered if he had.

Chapter Eighteen

WHEN I LEFT THE FEED store, I went home to drop off Maggie and the dog food. I needed to get to work. I had promised Sam I would make it in on time since Diane needed to leave for a dentist appointment right after the lunch hour rush. Business had been slow at the diner with the cold weather and I was sure I could handle things by myself.

"I've got to get going," Diane said. She had slung her big black bag over her shoulder and she had her keys in her hand. "Are you sure you'll be okay on your own?"

"Yeah, I've got it," I said, tucking my order book into my apron pocket. "If worse comes to worse, I can have Ron step in and bring drinks to the tables, or clear them. But honestly, I don't think we'll have many people this late in the day."

"Great, I'll talk to you later," she said.

"See ya," I said. It was one o'clock and there was one elderly gentleman in the corner, nursing a bowl of clam chowder. Sam's was only open for breakfast and lunch and we'd lock up as soon as the last customer left. Usually that was some time after 2:30, but it might be a lot earlier today.

I picked up a dishcloth and wiped down the front counter. It wouldn't take long to clean up this afternoon. I liked days like this, but I knew Sam would prefer the place to be hopping. The tourist season would pick up soon enough though. The Snake River was a big warm-weather draw.

The bell over the door jingled, and I looked up as Sarah Zumbro walked through it. She smiled. "Hi Rainey. Boy, it's quiet in here," she said, looking around the empty diner. "I guess that means I won't have to wait to be served."

I chuckled. "Icy streets make for a slow day. Would you like a booth?"

"No, I think I might just have a seat at the counter here and make things easier on you. I've been thinking about Sam's clam chowder. I hope you're not out."

I shook my head. "Nope, we've still got some simmering on the stove. I made some cornbread and honey butter earlier. Would you like a piece to go with it?"

"That sounds good," she said and took a seat at the counter. "And even though it's cold, I'd like some iced tea."

"You got it," I said and jotted down her order, then headed back to the kitchen to get her the clam chowder.

"A customer?" Sam asked hopefully.

"Yeah, she wants clam chowder. Easy peasy," I said and got a bowl out for the soup.

"Good, I can get cleaning the grill. I don't know if we'll have anyone else today," Sam said.

"Does that mean we'll close early?" I asked hopefully.

"Could be," he said and grinned. Sam was a good boss—low-key and drama free, just the way I liked things. Days like this were nice. They made up for how crazy things could get when the tourist season was in full swing. The Snake River recreation areas were Sparrow's claim to fame.

I cut a piece of cornbread and brought it with the clam chowder to Sarah. "Here we are. Let me get your iced tea."

"Thanks, Rainey," she said.

Heading back for the iced tea, I wondered about what Zack had said about Sarah. It had never set well with me that she hadn't reported her husband missing. And then there was the insurance money and a planned move across the country. I was suspicious of her and I thought Cade was too, although he sometimes didn't let me in on what he was thinking about a case.

"And here's the iced tea," I said and set the glass down in front of her. "Is there anything else I can get you?"

She shook her head. "No, this is fine. Hey Rainey, guess what I did yesterday?"

"What?" I asked, picking up the dishcloth again. Her eyes were lit up. She was happy about something.

"I gave my notice at school. I have a contract that I have to finish up but come June, I'm free as a bird," she said and giggled like a schoolgirl.

"Really? Well, that is great news! I bet you're counting the days."

"Ninety-three," she said and laughed. "I can hardly believe it! Granny was just wrong about me. I am not cut out to be a teacher, and I am going to do what I've always wanted to do. I can't wait!"

"Wow, so are you going to move to Massachusetts to be near your family?"

She nodded. "Yes. I've been thinking of all the things I need to do before I leave. I think I'm going to get rid of just about everything I own. I'll probably try to sell my furniture and most anything that's of any value. I can't see moving across the country and taking everything with me. I can buy new furniture and whatever I need once I get there."

"Well, that is exciting news, Sarah. I'm really happy for you. Will you be selling your home, too?"

"Yes, I'm putting it up for sale sometime in May. That way hopefully I won't have to wait too long after my last day of work to be able to move.

"I bet a place right on the lake will go fast," I said.

"I'm pretty sure it will. To be honest, I think I'll only get enough money out of it to pay off the mortgage, but that's fine. All the legal stuff should be done by then and I'll have the money from the life insurance and what's in Rob's bank account, so it will be fine." She picked up her glass of tea and took a sip.

"Are you sure? I would think a house out at the lake would sell for a lot," I said, leaning on the counter.

"Oh, I know it will," she said with a wave of her hand. "But we took out a second on our mortgage a couple of years ago. Unfortunately we owe the bank quite a lot. But, Rob had to have it. He wanted to pay off the credit cards and then he had to buy all that expensive fishing equipment." She shook her head. "He never was good with money. He liked to spend. I did not think it was a good idea to put all that debt on the house, but there's not much that can be done about it now."

"Really? I guess fishing equipment can get expensive?" I didn't pay a lot of attention to how much the equipment Cade used cost. I knew Cade loved it and appreciated expensive items, but I wasn't sure what he actually spent on it. I had bought him a fly-fishing rod for Christmas, and it had been more expensive than I realized it would be, but how much equipment could one man need?

"Well, it is when you buy everything new that comes out. He always had to have the newest of everything." She rolled her eyes and took a bite of her clam chowder. "Now this is what I'm talking about. Sam's clam chowder is the best."

"I wonder if you could sell some of his equipment? If it's top of the line stuff, seems like you could get some money out of it," I suggested.

She nodded. "I was thinking the same thing. I'm going to try to sell some of it online."

"Sarah, is some of his equipment missing?" I asked. It occurred to me that if she thought he was on a fishing trip, then he should have taken the best of his collection with him. Wouldn't she have noticed if he had left it all behind?

She stopped, her spoon halfway to her mouth. Her eyes went to mine. "You know, I never thought about that. I didn't notice. How silly of me."

That was odd. Here she had been so sure he was out fishing, and yet she hadn't noticed if he bothered to take his equipment with him?

"Seems like he'd take the best of the best with him if he was going to be a pro-angler," I said lightly.

She put her spoon down. "He has so much equipment, I seriously wouldn't be able to tell if he took any of it with him or not." She smiled, but it seemed like a nervous smile to me.

"I guess I could see that." I couldn't. If my husband had disappeared, and I thought there was a chance he was out fishing, I'd go over every piece of equipment he owned and try to figure out if he had taken some of it with him. Because if he wasn't actually fishing, then there was a reason to worry. And Sarah hadn't worried.

She stared at me. "I suppose you might think that I'm uncaring, but in my mind, I thought he was fishing and that he'd be back soon enough. I did care about my husband."

"Of course you do," I said looking at her levelly. I probably didn't sound like I thought so. In fact, I was pretty sure that I didn't sound like I thought that at all and I was pretty sure she didn't care.

She nodded. "Look, if that detective wants to talk to someone, he might try talking to Rob's uncle Barron. He came to my house three days ago asking for money. I told him I didn't have any."

"Why would he ask you for money?" I asked.

She shrugged. "He was always trying to get money from Rob. He thought he was entitled to it. I told Rob not to give him any, but Rob had a soft heart and he would give him money most of the time."

"What kind of money are we talking about? Twenty or thirty dollars? Or thousands?"

"Gosh no. Not thousands. I wouldn't stand for that. But he'd give him a hundred dollars. Maybe two hundred. When I told Barron I didn't have any money, he got mad. He told me it belonged to him and I owed it to him. Can you believe that? I think he'd been drinking. He has a history, you know."

"I've heard that. It sounds like maybe he had some problems managing his finances, but why would you think he killed Rob?" I asked.

"Because when I told him I wasn't giving him any money, he got mad. He said his money had been frozen, and he didn't have money to pay his rent."

"His money was frozen? What does that mean?"

She shrugged. "I don't know, but he asked me for a thousand dollars. No way was I giving him that kind of money just so he could spend it on booze. What do I care about whether he had the money to pay his rent? He lives at that old dilapidated boardinghouse across town, so it's not like his rent could be a thousand dollars. He just wanted money to blow, if you ask me. He can ask Rob's brothers to pay his bills, because I'm sure not going to do it."

I shrugged. "I guess you wouldn't care about whether he had the money to pay his rent."

"You're darn right," she said and took another bite of the clam chowder. "This is wonderful. Sam is a terrific cook."

"I'll let him know you said so. If you'll excuse me, I've got to get this place cleaned up," I said as I saw the elderly gentleman approach the cash register to pay for his meal.

"Hi Mr. Pemberton," I said and went to ring him up.

I wasn't convinced that either Zack or Sarah was innocent of Rob's murder. Even Barron and Kyle had a reason. I hoped Cade came up with the murderer soon. We had until June before Sarah would move to Massachusetts. I was reasonably sure it wouldn't take that long to figure out who the killer was, but an extradition would complicate things.

And that was when what Sarah said came to me. Barron's money had been frozen.

Chapter Nineteen

I WAS THANKFUL THAT we had a short day at the diner. I needed to speak to Barron. I tried calling Cade, but he didn't answer. I knew Barron lived at the boardinghouse and I decided I'd take a drive over there and see if he was around. I couldn't imagine the rent had to be terribly expensive at the boardinghouse and I wondered if he was telling the truth about needing money for rent. But maybe he was completely out of money and intended to spend the thousand dollars he told Sarah he needed to pay more than rent.

Sue Hester had owned the boardinghouse, but when she got into some trouble a few months earlier, her niece and her husband took it over. Sue had told me she didn't have any family, and for a time, it looked like the city would shut down the boardinghouse due to the owner abandoning the property. In a stroke of good fortune, her niece appeared the day before all of the boarders were going to have to vacate the premises. Most of the boarders were either completely alone in the world or made so little money that the boardinghouse was all they could afford.

I was pleased to see that the new owners were taking some pride in the place and had given the boardinghouse a facelift.

I hoped they were doing the same with the inside. Sue had allowed it to become fairly dilapidated in recent years.

When I pulled up to the boardinghouse, there was only one car out front, but that didn't surprise me. Most of the residents didn't own cars. They relied on the goodwill of others in the community or rode the local bus. The bus was fine for weekdays, but it didn't operate on the weekends.

I parked my car and then headed up the steps. I shivered when a memory of the last time I had been here crossed my mind. I hoped things had turned around here and that the residents were happy with the new owners.

I pushed open the front door and peered inside. The same worn carpet lined the foyer and hallway, but I could smell the faint scent of fresh paint. The cobwebs were missing as well as the coat of dust from the furniture and stairway. It was a definite improvement.

"Hi Harry," I said when I ran into Harry Adams in the hallway.

He stopped and looked at me, squinting his eyes, and then he snorted. "Hi yourself."

He shuffled on his way and I headed to the kitchen doorway. "Hi Annie," I said to the new proprietor.

She turned around and smiled when she saw me. "Hi Rainey. How are you?"

"Great. How are things going here? I noticed the new paint and gardening you all did outside. It looks great." By gardening, I meant that they had removed all the dead bushes that had lined the fence out front.

She grinned. "Thanks! We barely got the painting done before the weather turned. When it gets a little warmer, I told Gerald we need to put a new roof on the place. It leaks in some of the rooms upstairs. Thankfully, they're empty right now."

"That sounds like a job. I sure am glad you all are getting this place turned around," I said. "It's good for the residents as well as the community."

"It has been quite a job, I'll tell you," she said and chuckled. "We've started painting in some of the rooms, but it's going to take a while to get the entire inside done. Poor Gerald thinks I'm going to work him to death." She chuckled again.

"I bet he does," I said. "Annie, is Barron Zumbro around?"

"Sure, I think he's in his room. It's room six," she said. "Would you like to stay for dinner, Rainey? I'm putting a roast on right now."

"That's kind of you to ask Annie, but I don't think I'll be staying long, thanks."

"Okay, well one day you stop by and we'll have tea," she said.

"I'll do that," I said and headed down the hallway. Room six was the same room Silas Mills had stayed in before he died. To be honest, it made me feel a little creeped out that someone was living in there now, but I shook it off. I told myself it didn't mean a thing.

I knocked on the door and waited.

When Barron opened the door, he stared at me wide-eyed. "Well, hello. Rainey, is it? Or Stormy?"

I smiled and nodded. "It's Rainey. I hate to intrude Barron, but do you have a moment?" Now that I was here, I wondered if I had made a mistake. Barron was a quiet, older man, and I suddenly couldn't see him doing anything as terrible as killing his nephew.

"Why certainly, Rainey. Would you like to come in?"

I had already been in this room and it was small without any place to sit and talk comfortably. Besides that, it would be awkward to be in a man's bedroom when I barely knew him. "Maybe we could go to the dining room?"

He hesitated, then nodded. "Of course. It's gotten awfully cold out there, hasn't it?" he said as he stepped out and closed the door behind himself.

We walked to the dining room. There wasn't much privacy in the dining room, but I didn't feel comfortable in his room.

Annie turned to look at us as we passed through the kitchen.

"I hope you don't mind, but we're going to borrow the dining room for a few minutes," I said.

She smiled. "Not at all. Would you two like some tea? I've got a pot made."

"That sounds wonderful," I said. "I'll get it if you don't mind."

"You do that. I've got the cream and sugar," she said and brought a pitcher and sugar bowl to the table.

"Would you like to join us, Annie?" I asked. She had just suggested we have tea, and it seemed silly not to ask her. Besides that, I was suddenly unsure of how to ask Barron what I needed to ask. Another person in the room might help create a distraction should I need one.

"I'd like to, but I've got laundry to do. But I promise we will do it soon," she said and left the room.

I nodded and took a seat at the table across from Barron. "Let me pour you a cup of tea," I said. "I told my mother I ran into you a couple of weeks ago and she was so surprised. She said she hadn't seen you in years."

He chuckled. "I tell you, I've had it in mind to stop by the flower shop. Now I'm going to have to do it for sure."

"I'm sure she'd like that." I wasn't sure about that, but I was trying to find a way to ask him what I needed to know. "So Barron, how have you been getting along lately? You've been on my mind ever since you told me your nephew died."

He shrugged. "I'm doing the best I can. I do miss the boy. But that wife of his is an awful person. I don't know how he ever put up with her."

I looked at him. "Oh? Why do you say that?"

He gripped the teacup in his hand. "She—," he began and then stopped.

I looked at him expectantly. "She what?"

"Forgive me. It's just that I've run into a bit of financial difficulty. It isn't much, really. But I thought perhaps she could help me out since Rob had his inheritance. Rob would always help me out, you see. He understood what it's like for an elderly person like myself to struggle to make ends meet. It's not that I can't take care of myself, you understand, but sometimes I need a little help. But she refused to help me. My money has suddenly been frozen, and I only asked for a small loan to get me through until things could be straightened out."

"Oh, didn't you know?" I asked him.

"Know what?" he asked and took a sip of his tea.

"Rob was the only person on the bank account that had the inheritance money, and with his death, the bank froze the account. I would imagine it has to go through probate to be released and that could take months. It very well could be that she simply didn't have any money to give." I watched as his face went from surprise to anger.

"But she can get ahold of the money. She's his wife," he said. He clenched his teeth and then after a moment, with some effort, relaxed. "She froze the money."

I shook my head. "No. It doesn't matter that she's his wife. In fact, because Rob was murdered, I'm sure it will be a complicated drawn-out affair to get the money released."

He looked at me, surprised. "Do you really think so?"

"I do think so. There was a murder, and it's still unsolved, after all. I don't think the bank will release that money until they know who killed him." I didn't know if that was true or not, but I wanted to see his reaction.

"What about the insurance money? She had insurance on him. I know it was a lot of money. That woman wouldn't do anything on the cheap if it benefitted herself."

I nodded. "I doubt an insurance company is going to release the money until they know who killed Rob. It's a good thing Sarah has a job as a teacher, otherwise, I think money might be in short supply for her for a while."

He looked at me, his face blank. "I didn't think about that," he finally said.

"Tell me, Barron, how did you know the account was frozen?"

"What? What account?" he asked.

"Rob's bank account."

His cheeks went pink. "I didn't know his account was frozen. I just know that *my* money is frozen," he said slowly.

"Sarah said you knew. She said you came to her house and asked for money. She said that you said your money had been frozen, and you were unable to get to it, but that's odd that it would be frozen at the same time Rob's account had been frozen. Why do you think that is?"

He stared at me a few moments and then smiled. "My dear girl, I think you're mistaken. Let me go get my account statement. You sit right here," he said.

"Did you do it, Barron?" I asked him before he could stand up.

He narrowed his eyes at me and stood up. "You're something else, aren't you? You don't give up. What if I did? What if I went out onto the lake and hit him on the head with an oar?" he hissed. "I'm an old man. No one will believe it and there's no proof." He turned and hurried from the room.

My phone vibrated before I could get to my feet to go after him and I pulled it from my pocket. "Cade, I need you at the boardinghouse. Barron is the killer," I said when I answered it. I stood up and peered into the kitchen, but Barron was gone.

"Don't tell me you're there now," he said with a groan.

"Do you even need to ask?" I said. "He just confessed. Hurry." I hung up and put the phone back into my pocket and hurried down the hall to find Barron.

When I got to his room, the door was open, and it was empty. The hallway ended at a back door and it was open a crack. I ran to it and pulled it open. Barron was running across the snow. I was surprised at how far he had gotten in so short a time and I ran after him.

"Barron!" I called. He didn't look back. I watched as he ran across the backside of the property. "Barron!" I screamed when he suddenly disappeared from sight.

Chapter Twenty

I STOPPED IN MY TRACKS, my breath coming hard and heavy. I took one step, then another, then I broke into a trot, my eyes scanning the snow. If Barron was a magician, he was a good one. He had just pulled a disappearing act.

My feet slipped on the frozen earth before I saw the downward slope of the ground. The weather had turned warm several days earlier, and the snow had begun to melt, but yesterday the weather had turned frigid again making the ground a mass of slippery ice.

I lost my footing and landed on my behind, but it didn't stop my slide. I screamed and scrambled for purchase, but the ice was solid. The gaping hole that had suddenly appeared in the ground beckoned me and I screamed again. My foot hit a bump in the ground and I slid to a halt. I carefully looked over my shoulder. I estimated I was less than ten feet from the hole. I couldn't see how deep it was from where I lay, but Barron wasn't making any sound so I assumed it was deep.

Gingerly, I moved, rolling over onto my belly and pushed myself a few inches up the slope. The ground was slippery, and I said a silent prayer that I wouldn't end up in that hole. I didn't know how long it would take Cade to get here, but I thought it would be too long. My hand slipped as I tried to find something to grab hold of.

I decided it might be best to lay still and wait for Cade. I glanced over my shoulder again. "Barron?" I called. There was only silence in return. The cold made me shiver, and I wondered if I could keep my grip on the frozen ground long enough for Cade to get here.

"Rainey?" I heard someone say. I carefully looked up. Annie stood twenty feet from me.

"Don't come down here," I warned. "It isn't safe."

"I'll get Gordon," she said and turned and ran in the direction of the boardinghouse.

The seconds felt like hours as I dug my fingers into the ice to try to get a better grip. The ice felt like fire on my bare hands. From where I lay, I couldn't see the house. The angle was too steep and I couldn't risk craning my neck to look up. My body shook from the cold and from holding my muscles stiff to keep from slipping. I bit my lower lip to keep from crying.

"Rainey, hold on," I heard a voice say after what seemed like an eternity. I carefully moved my head to look up. Cade was there with a rope.

Chapter Twenty-One

"WOULD YOU LIKE SOME more tea?" Annie asked me.

I shook my head. "I think I just want to go home and take a hot shower." I pulled the blanket that was wrapped around me tighter and leaned in toward the fire. I didn't know if I would ever get warm again.

Cade appeared in the parlor doorway and I smiled. He walked over to me and put his arms around me. "I don't know what I'm going to do with you."

"Take me home so I can take a hot shower," I suggested.

"I'll call Stormy to come get you. I'll be here awhile."

"What happened to Barron?"

"The fire department is sending someone down into the hole in a harness to see if they can retrieve his body," he said, not letting me go.

I winced. "Annie said the hole was an abandoned well they found last fall."

"I know. Gordon said he was going to see about filling it in with gravel and sand, but it snowed before he had a chance. He was planning on having it done as soon as things thawed out."

I nodded. "I feel terrible," I said. "I didn't intend for this to happen."

"Don't. I was just looking through Barron's room and I found ATM receipts from a lot of different banks, as well as Rob's wallet."

I sighed. "That's what I thought. I swear, if I thought he was going to run, I never would have come over here. I just wanted to ask him some questions."

"I know. I'll have to finish up the investigation, but obviously, he killed Rob," he said. "I'll need an official statement from you."

I knew Cade was trying to make me feel better, but it wasn't working. I never would have wanted things to turn out this way. "Believe me, he killed Rob. I don't understand someone that's so cold-blooded. I don't think he had any remorse for what he'd done. He was so focused on the money."

"He made a lot of withdrawals from that account, so if he felt bad, it still didn't prevent him from taking the money."

I sighed. "When I asked him if he killed Rob, he said, what if he had gone out onto the lake in the rowboat and hit him in the head with an oar? He said no one would believe an old man would do that and there wasn't any proof."

"We were still waiting on the DNA from the rowboat, including what looked like blood on one of the oars. I'm pretty sure we do have the proof, and a judge wouldn't care one bit if he was old," he said.

I nodded. "It's a sad affair when one family member kills another."

He kissed the top of my head. "I don't want to lose you. You have got to quit getting into trouble," he said.

I looked at him. "Maybe I should have made that my New Year's resolution."

"Haha. Yes, that would have been nice. For now, I'm calling Stormy. I'll come see you as soon as I get free, but it will probably be tomorrow."

I nodded and shivered. I never wanted to see ice again for as long as I lived.

The End

Sneak Peek

Cupcakes and a Murder
   A Rainey Daye Cozy Mystery, book 10
Chapter One

"I would kill for one of those cupcakes," Arnold Singer said. He was stooped over, looking into the glass-covered display case, his eyes glued to the plate full of cupcakes I had just placed in it. He licked his lips, his eyes never leaving the cupcakes

I smiled, trying not to laugh. "They do look good, don't they?" I asked. "I got up early this morning to make them, but you don't have to kill for them. They'll only set you back a dollar."

He straightened up and narrowed his eyes at me. "Only a dollar?" he asked suspiciously. "That's all?"

I nodded. "I'm trying out cupcake recipes for my new cookbook. The only catch is that I need your opinion on them after you've tried one. I like constructive criticism, so don't hold back. If they're missing something, or they're too sweet, I need to know. I can't publish a cookbook with recipes that aren't as perfect as I can make them."

He licked his lips again, his eyes on the chocolate cherry cupcakes. Arnold was our mailman, and he still held the diner's mail in his hand, apparently forgetting it was what he came in for.

He looked at me. "I'm not supposed to spend any money this week," he said sadly. "My wife keeps a tight hold on the checking account, and she warned me three times this morning that this is a no-spend week." His eyes went to the cupcakes again, and he sighed.

Call me a soft touch, but I felt sorry for him. He really wanted a cupcake. "Well then, how about I just give you one?"

His eyes lit up. "Really? You can do that?"

I nodded, still trying to suppress a chuckle. Arnold was in his late forties, short, and what could best be described as portly. His close-cropped black hair was receding in front, and his skin had a perpetually pink tone. "Sure, I can do that. I made them, after all. Which one do you want?"

He grinned, his thin lips stretching over his teeth. "I really couldn't ask you to do that. It wouldn't be right," he said, shaking his head.

"Arnold, I made these cupcakes primarily to get peoples' opinions on them. We're only charging a dollar because I need to buy ingredients to make more of them as I continue to work on the recipe. Believe me, even at a dollar each, it will be more than enough money to buy more ingredients. Giving one away isn't going to leave me short. What I really want is input on them. I need that more than the money. Just promise to come back tomorrow and let me know how you liked it."

He grinned. "You're the best, Rainey! I have to deliver the mail anyway, so I can stop in tomorrow and tell you how it was. I'd like that one," he said, pointing to the fattest one in the bunch. The batter was cherry flavored, and it had chocolate frosting, cherry cream cheese filling, and a candied cherry sat on the top. I then topped it off with a drizzle of cherry syrup.

"You got it," I said and handed him the cupcake. "You'll need some napkins." I held out three napkins to him.

He licked his lips and took the cupcake and napkins from me with his free hand. "You're the best, Rainey!" he said again. "This looks delicious."

I chuckled. "Thanks, Arnold. You can come and get a cupcake from me anytime. Just don't forget to stop back in and tell me what you think."

"You know I will. I'll see you tomorrow morning when I deliver the mail." He looked down at the mail he still held in his other hand. "Oh. I guess I better give you this."

"Thanks, Arnold," I said, taking the handful of mail from him. "I'll see you tomorrow."

"You got it, Rainey," he said and headed to the front door, whistling.

I looked through the mail he handed me and went back to the kitchen. My boss, Sam Stevens, was at the grill flipping pancakes.

"You're a soft touch, Rainey," he said over his shoulder.

"I know, I know. Arnold is a good guy, and he really wanted one of those cupcakes. I couldn't deprive him."

"Anything exciting in the mail?" he asked without turning around. Sam owned Sam's Diner and was a mellow boss to work for. His hair was growing too long again, and he wore it in a hair net these days.

"Only if you call the electric bill, a clothing catalog, and a grocery store flyer exciting," I said. "You might need to look elsewhere for excitement."

He snorted. "That electric bill will probably excite me, but in a bad way."

"I bet. I'll set it all on your desk," I said and headed to his office. Sparrow, Idaho hosted a busy tourist season during more temperate months with the Snake River drawing people to the excellent local fishing and camping. The diner was usually hopping during the tourist season, but winter had put a damper on things. We'd had a break in the weather the previous week, but it had turned cold again. I missed the blue skies of spring and summer.

"I see cupcakes," Diane Smith, the other waitress on duty said happily when I emerged from the office.

"You sure do. You better get one before they're all gone," I said. I was writing an Americana themed cookbook, and I frequently brought dishes for my co-workers to try out. Some of the food was sold and sometimes given, to customers. It allowed me to receive feedback on the food I made, and it was a big help in perfecting the recipes.

"Thanks, I need one. I skipped breakfast. If my kids saw me eat a cupcake this early, they'd point their fingers and tell me I'm not allowed to have sweets for breakfast, but I'm going to get one anyway," she said and headed back to the front counter. "Just don't tell them!"

"I promise not to tell," I said as I followed her back out front.

"Save one for me!" Ron White, our dishwasher called from his place near the sink.

"You got it!" I called back to him.

"What kind do we have here?" she asked, opening the display case.

"There's chocolate, cherry, and chocolate cherry," I said. "I think I'm going to make some lemon ones next. I've been craving lemon."

"I love lemon," she said, picking up a chocolate cherry cupcake. "Don't forget to bring them to work so I can try one."

"You know I will," I said. Diane was one of my favorite people to work with. She was in her mid-forties and had been waitressing all her life. She was a professional, and I could always count on her to more than pull her own weight when things got busy.

The bell above the door jingled and my boyfriend, Detective Cade Starkey, walked in. He smiled at me and headed over to the front counter and sat down. "What's up, buttercup?"

I chuckled and leaned over the counter and kissed him. "Nothing."

"Hi Diane," he said, leaning to the side to see her standing behind me.

"Hi, Cade. Look what I got," she said and held up the cupcake for him to see. She had taken a bite and the cherry filling was visible.

"Don't tease me. I want one of those," he said looking at me.

"Well, pick one out," I said, indicating the display case.

He stood up and looked at the cupcakes. "I want one like she's got."

I got him one of the cherry chocolate cupcakes and set it in front of him. "I'll get you some coffee," I said and headed to the coffee pot. I heard the bell jingle over the door, and Diane greeted the customers that came into the diner.

"Wow," Cade said, his mouth full of the cupcake when I returned with his coffee.

I set the cup in front of him. "Is it any good?"

He made a circle with his finger and thumb, nodding, and took another bite. "The best," he said after he swallowed.

"Well you better order some protein to go with that, or you're going to end up with low blood sugar," I warned. "Sugar on its own this early isn't good for you."

"Yes, Ma'am," he teased and saluted me. "How about scrambled eggs and toast?"

I chuckled. "For some weird reason, I knew you were going to say that. It's like I'm psychic or something," I said and pulled my order book from my apron pocket and jotted down his order. Cade was a man of few tastes in the morning. Scrambled eggs and toast were his usual fare.

"You're a genius," he said and took a sip of his coffee. "Boy, this cupcake is good."

"Thanks." I headed back to the kitchen with the order ticket. "Sam, Cade's here," I said.

"Scrambled eggs and white toast it is," he said without looking at the order.

I hung the ticket up anyway. "There are a couple more customers out there, so maybe things are going to pick up today."

"I hope so. I've been considering discontinuing the clam chowder for a while. Even with the smaller pots I've been making, we've had leftovers."

"Maybe you should completely scale down the menu during the winter," I suggested. "Just make the items that sell the most and advertise that that's what you're doing so people know they can still get their favorites, but not some of the other items."

"I had the same idea. March will be here soon, and business usually picks up toward the end of the month. Maybe I'll plan to do that next year. That will give me plenty of time to let people know," he said, cracking eggs into a bowl.

"That's a great idea," I said and popped two slices of bread into the toaster.

"Hey Rainey, will you make chocolate turtle cupcakes next?" Ron asked as he rinsed a plate and set it in the drying rack.

"That sounds good. I don't think I've ever made turtle cupcakes before," I said. "I'm going to have to look into that."

"See? I've got good ideas," he said without looking at me. "You could pay me in cupcakes for those ideas."

"I might just do that, Ron." When Cade's breakfast was ready, I took it out to him and set it down on the counter. "Here we are."

"Mmm, Scrambled eggs and toast," he said, picking up his fork.

I glanced over at the display case. "Wait a minute, something's not right here," I said. Four cupcakes were missing from the cake stand. "Let's see, I gave Arnold a cupcake, Diane took one, and you took one. And yet, four cupcakes are missing from the display."

"I don't know what you're talking about," he said as he scooped eggs onto a piece of toast.

I narrowed my eyes at him. "I think you do."

The door swung open before I could accuse him of eating two cupcakes. "Hello folks," I said to the party of three that walked through the door.

Buy Cupcakes and a Murder on Amazon:

https://www.amazon.com/gp/product/B07QLGRPBJ

If you'd like updates on the newest books I'm writing, follow me on Amazon and Facebook:

https://www.facebook.com/
Kathleen-Suzette-Kate-Bell-authors-759206390932120/

https://www.amazon.com/Kathleen-Suzette/e/B07B7D2S4W/
ref=dp_byline_cont_pop_ebooks_1

Made in the USA
Monee, IL
26 February 2025

12967706R00090